POVERTY CRUSADE:

A little African village's
campaign against world poverty

POVERTY CRUSADE:

A little African village's campaign against world poverty

R. Peprah-Gyamfi

Perseverance Books Ltd

POVERTY CRUSADE:
A little African village's campaign against world poverty

Published by **Perseverance Books**
Loughborough
Leicestershire
UK

email: **info@peprah-gyamfi.com**

ISBN: 978-1-913285-00-5

www.peprah-gyamfi.com

Speak up for those who cannot speak for themselves, for the rights of all who are destitute. Speak up and judge fairly; defend the rights of the poor and needy.
Proverbs 31:8-9 (NIV).

Dedication

This book is dedicated to the poor, destitute and impoverished, those who among other things are forced to retire to bed hungry, for lack of resources; to dwell in dilapidated, squalid and appalling homes in filthy, overcrowded and dreadful slum settlements such as *Agbogbloshie* in Accra, Manila North Cemetery in the Philippines and Ciudad Nez, Mexico City, Mexico; to sleep rough in freezing and biting cold winters on the streets of New York, London, Moscow, etc.

You and I can only hope and pray that a day will dawn in the not distant future when mankind will learn to set his priorities right and place the need to undertake immediate steps to rid the world of abject poverty high above that of investing trillions upon trillions of precious US dollars in weapons of mass destruction and research aimed at the discovery of life on far, far distant planets!

Table of Contents

Foreword

This is surely an inspired work that is both a fantasy as well as a polemical dream rooted in reality! The author, Dr Robert Peprah-Gyamfi, was born in a remote little village called Mpintimpi in Ghana before he made his way, by sheer determination and faith, to Germany, where he qualified as a medical doctor, before he continued on to England where he still practises as a doctor. But he has also written many books that are testimonies of his faith and his love for Ghana, especially the poor and needy in the little village of his birth. That village, Mpintimpi, becomes here, in this much-needed book about finding solutions for world poverty, an emblem, a typical example, of the human condition, of human rights that are withheld not only by the world's wealthy countries, but by the corrupt politicians at the helm of the very countries wherein villages like Mpintimpi exist. So, in a sense, the author, as a crusader for human rights, has placed Mpintimpi on the world map!

The author is careful to explain, at the outset, that this book is the outcome of a dream, where imagination takes the reader before the leaders of the Western world, where meetings and interviews with Angela Merkel, Theresa May, the Queen and, the controversial *pièce de résistance* himself, Donald Trump! These imagined interviews will surprise the reader – not only are they convincing in the way the author has captured their attitudes, but some of their replies to the searching questions put to them are surprisingly cogent in themselves! The result is a debate where each party, each side, as it were, puts forward convincing and relevant points. President Trump's proposal for a "deal", however, is typically outrageous and laughable!

There is an abundance of humour, too, that makes this work a delight to read. We see the Western world with its modern technological marvels – great airliners, underground trains, massive supermarkets – through the eyes of three delegates from Mpintimpi, who have never been away from their little village. Adwoa, an endearing crippled woman, poor but proud, undercuts the false pride of security officers, or flight attendants, when she flies for the first time. In Berlin she insists on carrying her shopping on her head, as she did in her village, much to the consternation of the locals! In England she cuts through the outward trappings of the Prime Minister and finds herself in Buckingham Palace, curtsying before the Queen of England! (Here we learn a lot about protocol when approaching the monarch – useful tips if anyone should find themselves in the royal presence!)

I suppose you could call the book a wish-fulfilment dream, for it culminates with a march against poverty, hosted by the United Nations, in New York! We the readers are swept along with the dream, and listen to the various speeches, that becomes the essence for the case against world poverty, and the plea for a world benefit and health organisation. Let us come together, is the author's concluding plea, to join our efforts towards helping the millions of the poor of this world. It's a dream of a new Utopia, of a united world that works together for the benefit of humanity worldwide.

Charles Muller
MA (Wales), PhD (London),
DEd (SA), DLitt (UFS)

Acknowledgements

My heartfelt thanks go to God Almighty, for imparting the wisdom needed to write this book.

Rita, my wife, together with our children Karen, David, and Jonathan, also deserve my thanks and appreciation for their support and encouragement, which enabled me to persevere to the successful conclusion of this work.

I am also grateful to Dr Charles Muller of Diadembooks.com for the excellent copy editing of the manuscript and for writing an illuminating foreword.

PROLOGUE

Thought-provoking final words of a departing one

On April 10, 2018, I returned home from work on a cold, rainy day to receive a call from my sister Manu from Mpintimpi, the little village in Ghana where I was born, informing me about the passing away of one of the residents of the little settlement a few days before. The individual who had passed away happened to be Moses Kwasi Agyei Sarkodie, known by everyone in the village as Moses, for short. Moses was one of my closest companions at the time I was growing up in the little settlement, which lies about 150 kilometres to the north-west of Accra, Ghana's capital. Even after moving to Europe, I kept in regular contact with my childhood and boyhood friend.

A brilliant fellow, Moses could without doubt have made it far in his academic journey had his parents been able to afford to finance his education beyond the elementary school stage. Unfortunately, they could not, forcing him to nip in the bud his dream of pursuing his education up to university level.

For the last several years he had been battling with insulin-dependent diabetes. In the end he succumbed to complications from the chronic disease.

What, according to the account of my sister, turned out to be the final words of my departed friend as he battled with death, occupied my mind for several days after the news was broken to me.

Manu told me on the phone that, as my good friend wrestled with the awful disease surrounded by his close family members, just as he was about to give up the ghost, he murmured:

"Someone please contact Manu [my sister] and ask her to inform Peprah [me] that I am about to embark on a journey, so he should come over and see me off!"

Just as those words passed his lips, he is said to have shut his eyes for good!

That my closest companion had chosen to direct his last words on Earth to no one else but me, someone he had not seen for almost three years, someone who happened to be in the UK thousands of kilometres away from his deathbed, occupied my thoughts for some time.

In the Twi language,[1] my vernacular, to see off someone embarking on a journey means, literally, to pay for that individual's journey, or at least provide the person involved with some pocket money for the trip!

Though I did not have to pay for the journey of the departed one, that was not the end of the matter!

In the first place there were costs related with his burial and funeral that needed to be met. In our culture the responsibility fell not only on his widow but also on members of his extended family. I was aware that all the parties involved were struggling to make ends meet financially. Even without the last spoken words of my departed friend, I would have contributed towards meeting the costs associated with his death. The last spoken words of my close pal placed an added responsibility on me to ensure that a fitting burial was organised for him.

---

[1]   The language of the Akan population group of Ghana.

Beside contributing generously for his burial, I also recognised in his final words the need to help pay for the upbringing of his two little children. It is superfluous for me to mention here that his impoverished widow was not in a position to do so.

The dire financial situation of the widow and children of my departed friend occupied my mind throughout the evening.

The thoughts did not leave me as I retired to bed that night. Instead, as I lay down waiting for sleep to overtake me, I ruminated, yes agonised, over not only the precarious financial situation of his widow, but also of the residents of the little village of my birth in general.

Through my regular mobile phone contact with them, I was aware of the dire financial predicament of the populace.

Not that the situation was new! No, indeed ever since I was big enough to understand my environment, I have been witness to the day-to-day struggle of the residents to keep themselves above water financially.

I remember Mother, during her lifetime, on almost a daily basis, imploring Almighty God to help her find the means to feed herself and her eight children. As far as we were concerned, the Lord's prayer "Give us this day our daily bread" was not simply a prayer recited by way of daily routine. No, we needed Heaven on a daily basis, literally, to lead us to our meals.

Though we were not threatened with starvation, the poor financial situation of my parents meant we lived virtually from hand to mouth. Any condition, like disease, that rendered one or both of them incapable of cultivating the land in a particular year could lead to food shortage. This is because they did not have the means to purchase food from the market to offset, even for the very short term, what we did not grow ourselves.

The same applied to other residents of the village.

Indeed, as far as their financial capabilities go, virtually nothing has changed in the fortunes over the years. Instead, they struggle through life the very hard way, from the rising of the sun to its setting. In previous times those who, by way of disease, disability, old age, etc., were unable to fend for themselves were helped by extended family members. My understanding is that, due to the rising cost of living, family members were increasingly unwilling or unable to shoulder the burden. With virtually no form of a state-operated benefit system in place, such individuals without doubt are in a very bad situation.

A Twi saying has it that "one carries into one's dream the things that are before one's eyes". Did I indeed carry into my dream the things that occupied my mind as I lay in bed waiting for sleep to descend on me and take over my being – if only temporarily?

That may well have been the case. Whatever the case, though, the fact remains that in the course of the night I experienced a series of scenarios, visions, images, visual flashes that, while featuring the residents of Mpintimpi in the centre stage, unfolded in various parts of the globe.

I may well have been in a dream. If it were indeed a dream, it was a peculiar one, for sure, beyond anything I have experienced over the period of more than half a century during which I have called planet Earth my home.

On coming back to myself, I immediately switched on my laptop to record the bullet points of this extraordinary experience.

Due to the pressure of everyday life – related to family life, work and other commitments of daily life – it has taken me almost a year to find the time to write a detailed report of the extraordinary experience.

I want to stress the fact that whatever is recorded in the pages of this book never actually occurred in real life. I can only appeal to the individuals, organisations, corporate bodies, etc., that are mentioned in the account, to refrain from dragging me before a court of law to sue me for libel, defamation, misrepresentation, vilification or for anything else that would otherwise be a breach of the law by dint of me putting words into their mouths.

Having said this by way of introduction, I invite the reader to accompany me on a journey through my extraordinary dream experience.

1

The unending sufferings of a forgotten community

In my dream I happened to have made an unannounced visit to Mpintimpi. Though I had intended to keep my visit secret, somehow word of my presence quickly spread through the little settlement.

On hearing about my presence, almost the entire village population descended on our home. They were there not only to welcome me, but also to seek my assistance concerning various problems plaguing them.

At that juncture, scenes from a visit a few years before flashed through my mind. On that occasion, I was not visiting alone but with my whole family – Rita, my wife, and our three children, Jonathan, David and Karen. The villagers confronted us with all sorts of problems, problems that, to be fair to them, were not feigned. Among others, they brought to our attention various kinds of disease conditions, some life-threatening, that they had until then kept to themselves for lack of money to bring to the attention of doctors.

Others requested me to help them pay their children's school fees, repair the roofs of homes that had been torn apart by a recent storm that had caused considerable damage in the community, and to help them feed themselves due to a poor harvest, etc.

The "social consultation hours", as I dubbed them, went on for several hours.

Karen, who was visiting Africa for the first time and was unfamiliar with the local culture whereby extended family members who are deemed in a position to do so are expected to help others in need, was amazed to find me dish out money to one individual after the other!

"Hey, Papa, why are you dishing your money out to everyone?" she asked, quite upset. "Surely your generosity amounts to committing financial suicide!"

Did I previously state that one was expected to help family members? Well, in our little community where everyone knew each other, such expectations on me were not restricted to family members. Instead, other community members expected "one of their own" who had managed to excel in life to help them as well. And that is exactly what happened, as almost everyone in the village took advantage of my presence to seek my assistance.

For the sake of space and also in order not to bore the reader with details of every problem presented to me in what turned out to be a dream, I am only citing a few examples.

One of the residents arrived with her medical report in her hand. Prior to handing it to me, she told me her story:

"It began with loss of appetite which resulted in time with weight loss. In due time I also noticed a gradual distension of my belly. After trying traditional medicine without any improvement, I took a loan and sought help in the next available hospital about 30 kilometres away. After the tests I was handed a report and asked to purchase some medicine."

Saying that, she handed the sheet to me. Printed boldly on it was – *Hepatitis B positive*!

A closer look revealed she had been diagnosed with chronic hepatitis B infection, something that could require a long-term or even lifelong treatment and regular tests to monitor the state of her liver.

"Your doctor has without doubt explained your condition to you. It is a liver disease. It can be life-threatening so you have to undergo treatment as already prescribed."

"*Kudi?*"

"What do you mean by '*kudi*'?"

"Hello! Have you been so long away from home to forget one of the popular slangs for money!"

"No, I haven't. I just said, '*kudi*', and so what?"

"That's is why I am here – looking for *kudi!*"

"But I am not a bank! Go to the bank for *kudi!*"

"All jokes aside – Doc, I need your help. The doctor told me I will need to take medicine for at least six months. According to him I will need to spend 200 Ghana cedis (approximately $40.00) per month on the tablets. Just about the same amount will be required for blood tests and his consultation fees. Then comes money to pay for transportation to Nkawkaw, which, as you are aware, is about 30 kilometres away.

"It will take me more than two years to save that amount of money from my meagre earnings from the sale of crops from my farm. I am still trying to raise a loan – with little success, so far."

Next I would like to mention the case of an insulin-dependent diabetic who came to plead for assistance.

"Doc, please do what you can to help. I don't have the means to purchase insulin on a regular basis. This has forced me to resort to the practice of fasting as a way of controlling my insulin."

"Resorting to fasting to control your blood sugars? How do you do that?"

"I have conditioned my brain to monitor my blood sugar in this way: I usually get the feeling when my blood sugar is dropping. When it comes to a point when I get the feeling it has dropped too low, I eat something to raise it."

"How can you tell if it gets too high?"

"It hardly happens! We don't have food in abundance here, so the temptation to eat in excess does not arise!"

The third case involved a resident who was plagued with severe arthritis concerning both knees. She had to resort to a walking stick to take a few steps from her room to the outside to enjoy fresh air. The doctors had requested her to return for tests to help them decide on possible surgery – as with the case of the resident with the liver condition who failed to turn up for financial reasons.

Not only in the matter of their health were they struggling to make ends meet. Inadequate rains during the previous planting season had led to food shortages. Though the situation could not be described as a full-blown famine, as I learnt from them, many of them had to struggle to come by more than one meal per day.

The effect of the food shortage was evident in the features of those who contacted me and those I met on the street – most appeared among other things to be underweight and displayed prominent collar bones and ribs.

Much as I was happy to do all I could to help, the hard reality as to the limit I could go to soon dawned on me.

What was to be done? Leave them to their fate? I wish indeed I could! There is a Twi saying, *"wani anhu a enye tane"* – which I can only approximately translate into English as follows: "It is only when one does not become witness to something [for example suffering], that one can remain aloof to it."

My eyes had seen the suffering; I was feeling the pain and could not remain aloof to it. Yet much as I was desirous of helping relieve the pain, there was a limit to what I could do. What then? Leave them to battle things on their own? Abandon the woman battling with a hepatitis infection to her fate to await the likely outcome of her condition – certain death?

"You cannot do that!" a voice within me protested.

4

"What then?" I countered with my own voice.

Suddenly an idea flashed through my mind – bring their plight before the president of the country! He did not give birth to them, certainly; but he was nevertheless the head of state in the country. The state is responsible for the well-being of its citizens. He was the president of the country, thus the final point of contact for its suffering population, I reasoned.

Though I had been absent from the country, I had followed online how, during the election campaign ahead of the elections that brought his party to power almost 18 months before, his party had promised to do whatever it takes, once in power, to help end abject poverty in the country. One and a half years had passed since his party assumed the reigns of office. With no sign of the promised improvement in their living conditions in sight, it was high time for the residents of the community to call on him to remind him of those promises.

Having made up my mind, I decided to travel with a delegation to present a petition to the president.

I couldn't do so of my own volition, though. As with any matter concerning the village as a whole, it had to receive the blessings of the head of the community, the traditional leader or chief. He occupies a special stool, the symbol of power and authority. In almost every community in the country a particular extended family clan is custodian of the stool of authority of the settlement. Only members of that particular extended family have the right of occupancy.

Moments later, I was on my way to the Ahenfie, meaning literally "Chief's residence", to inform him about my plans.

The idea was well received by Nana Kofi Du Ampem IV, our respected leader.

In my presence he summoned the gong-gong beater, the individual responsible for announcing to the community any important news or anything in keeping with tradition he felt the need to inform them of, into his presence. He arrived a short while later.

"Take your gong and go around the streets and ask all committee members to assemble here tomorrow at 8 o'clock for an important meeting", the traditional leader told him.

"Your word is my command, your Highness", he replied, bowing before the chief.

Moments later I begged permission to leave. As I stepped onto the street, I could hear the beating of the gong – *Kon-kon; kon-kon; kon-kon* – followed by the screaming of the beater: "Fellow residents of Mpintimpi, I send you greetings from Nana. He is requesting members of the Village Town Committee to meet at his residence tomorrow at 8 o'clock in the morning for an important meeting. No lateness will be tolerated." *Kon-kon; kon-kon; kon-kon*, he beat his gong again to signify the end of the message he was carrying.

From there he moved a distance of about 50 metres and repeated the announcement.

***

The committee met the next day as planned. On hearing what the chief had to say, some members opined it would be better, initially, to channel their grievances through the member of parliament for the area rather than travel the distance to the presidency in Accra.

The dissenting voices were in the minority, however. The majority agreed with the traditional leader and me that the time for waiting was over. The local MP had been representing them for over six years. Having failed in that period to make any difference, it was time to take matters into their own hands and petition the ultimate authority in the country.

Having agreed on the need to send the delegation, the issue that needed to be settled was who and how many to send.

Concerning the number, I made it known to them I was prepared to sponsor a maximum of three delegates; they were of course free to pay for additional delegates. The matter of the number to send was quickly settled for obvious reasons.

It was when it came to the selection that the discussion turned turbulent – almost everyone, including those who were initially against the idea – wanted to accompany me to see the president in person.

Readers will recall I mentioned earlier that the chief has the final say in matters relating to affairs. Tradition does not permit him to speak directly to his subjects. He does so through his *Okyeame*, a linguist.

Just as things seemed to be getting out of hand, he summoned his *Okyeame* to call for order.

Absolute silence soon returned to the hall. Next, he called the *Okyeame* to come up close to him and murmured something in his ear.

He then stepped before the gathering and began:

"This is what His Highness has asked me to convey to the gathering:

"Concerning the delegates: two names came spontaneously into my mind – Kofi Botwe, also known by all as Kwootwe, and Douglas Akwasi Abankwah, known by all as Douglas, for short.

"Since both are men, fairness demands that we select a woman to accompany them. I have no one in mind so I will leave the decision to the committee."

After proposals and counter-proposals from some of those assembled, the committee finally agreed on Adwoa Koramah.

At this juncture, I should like to provide the reader with a short profile of each of the three delegates.

Papa Kofi Botwe (Papa is the title for any elderly male in the community; in case of a female the term *Maame* is employed): Kwootwe, as he was known by all, was the most elderly male citizen of the village. Indeed, apart from his sister Maame Afia Mera, who is two years his senior, no one in the settlement surpassed him in age. Aged about 80 (his exact age was not recorded) he had spent almost his entire life in the little village. Like almost every adult resident of the village, he had spent most of his life tilling the land. Apart from growing food crops to sustain himself and his family, he cultivated cocoa on about an acre of land that served as a source of income for him and his family. Though meagre, the income so obtained kept them going. Then came the year 1983 when the country was visited by bush fires that spread to various parts of the country. Luck was not on his side; his entire cocoa farm was razed by the fire.

Since then he had been left with virtually no source of income. At the age of 80, and with his strength failing, he was at the mercy of other members of his extended family and the community at large to survive.

Douglas Akwasi Abanquah, without doubt, was one of the most enlightened residents of the little village. After finishing his elementary education, he did three years further study in a commercial college, qualifying in the end as an accountancy clerk.

He eventually moved from his native Oboh, a medium-sized town in the Eastern Region of the country, to take up a position as an accountancy clerk in Accra, about 100 miles to the south.

About two years in his new role, he got a call one day from his maternal grandmother. She had acquired a large track of farmland in the little village called Mpintimpi, about 40 miles to the south-west of Obo. She was inviting him, the most elderly male member of the family, to move from Accra to the village to cultivate the land!

Many a young man in his position might well have refused to give up the comfortable life of Accra in exchange for that of a little village that boasted no electricity or pure drinking water. Not so Douglas. Instead he decided to take up the challenge and do the bidding of his grandma. That was about 40 years ago.

Though he had in the meantime managed to cultivate cocoa on about two acres of his farmland, he never ceased to lament the lack of concern of the government for the poor farmers. At the same time that his responsibilities were increasing (his six children needed to be educated), the yields from his farm were falling. He was embittered because, despite the fact that cocoa brought the larger share of Ghana's foreign exchange earnings, not much attention was paid to those who cultivate it. Not surprisingly therefore he saw this call as a golden opportunity to let out his pent-up anger, not specifically against the present head of state, but against almost all of the others who had ruled the country since independence.

Adwoa Koramah: what a tragic life hers has been! Affectionately called Adwoa by all, her life story has all the ingredients needed to melt even a heart of steel.

As the story goes, at the time when she was barely five years old, she developed a high fever. Unable to afford both the transportation to hospital and the expected hospital bill, her parents sought help from a quack doctor who had made a stop at the village. The quack doctors of that time! One could write a horror story about them! Though unlicensed to do so, they went about in the rural areas practising their trade.

Though they carried tablets, suppositories, syrups, ointments, creams, etc., in their "doctor's bags", they were best known for what came to be known as "smuggle injections". They took advantage of the prevailing belief amongst the general population concerning the effectiveness of injections and administered them to their patients, irrespective of their symptoms and complaints.

Adwoa might probably have been afflicted by malaria.[2] Yet the visiting "doctor" saw the need to administer an injection. In the end "the health care professional" injected the medicine directly into one of the sciatic nerves, two of the main nerves of the body, each responsible for supplying a leg. That led to the complete paralysis of the affected left leg.

Unable to afford even a proper pair of crutches, the parents went into the woods, cut a stick just about her height and presented it to her as a walking aid. With it, she hopped from one place to the other, supporting herself on only the right leg.

Elsewhere one would have thought about physiotherapy. It is superfluous to mention here that such a facility was not available in our little village. Disuse of her left leg led to the shrinking of the muscles. In the end, one could hardly differentiate between the size of her left disabled leg and that of her wooden walking aid, which was barely 10cm in diameter!

Several years later, a Good Samaritan visiting the village, on seeing her condition, donated a single elbow crutch, which she has since then been using.

---

[2] Malaria is widespread in our part of the world, a condition that could have been treated with a syrup.

2

Valuable connections and links of a grandson turned politician

How could ordinary citizens from rural Mpintimpi get an appointment at the seat of government, indeed an appointment with the most powerful man of the republic in his imposing presidential palace in Accra?

As the committee deliberated the matter, someone in the group came up with the idea of seeking the help of Frank. Why hadn't that idea flashed through my mind earlier! Indeed, Frank was the only person known to us who could help establish a link with the seat of government.

Being the son of Amma, who happens to be the daughter of my late brother, Emmanuel, he would normally be called my great-nephew. Not so in our Akan culture. Indeed, in our culture, the daughter of my brother is not considered my niece but rather has the status of my daughter. It will indeed be considered contemptuous on my part not to regard her as a daughter.

Following on that logic, Frank, the son of my daughter Amma, is my grandson, and not my great-nephew. I better not delve any further into the intricate Akan external family relationships so as not to confuse those not familiar with them.

One may as well regard Frank as someone who has walked in the footsteps of his grandfather, for, having grown up in the humble surroundings of Mpintimpi, he also managed to make it all the way to the Cape Coast University. After graduation, he secured a job as a secondary school teacher.

Even during his time at university, he became actively involved in politics and joined the New Patriotic Party (NPP). He played an active role in the election campaign of the party in his constituency in the December 2016 elections that brought his party from opposition into power.

Was it a way of thanking him for his dedication to his party? I cannot say for sure, but the fact remains that not long after his party had assumed power, he was appointed personal assistant to a top civil servant in Accra. He wholeheartedly accepted the new position and moved to the capital.

Moments after the idea was floated in the presence of the assembly, I extracted my phone from my pocket and dialled his number. Soon the link was established. Unaware of my sudden and unannounced visit to the village, he initially thought I was calling from my home in the UK.

"No, I am not in the UK, I am visiting Mpintimpi", I told him.

"Visiting Mpintimpi? When did you arrive?"

"Yesterday!"

"You usually keep us informed of your visits long before they take place; what has brought you back home at such short notice?"

"I will let you know later."

"Okay; that's fine Grandpa!"

A short silence followed, broken by me.

"We need your help."

"You and who?"

"The residents of Mpintimpi!"

"In what way?"

"We want to send a delegation to meet the president."

"To meet the president! Are you kidding, Grandpa?"

"No, we mean business."

"You and who?"

"The Mpintimpi Village Committee."

"Really?!"

"We are sending a delegation to present our petition to the president."

"Petition?"

"Yes."

"What is it about?"

"About issues pertaining to the hardships faced by the residents."

"But I thought our honourable member of parliament is the first point of contact in such matters."

"Well, Frank, I am speaking on behalf of the Village Committee. We are gathered before the chief. I have put the phone on speaker so you have to mind your words; any insolent behaviour on your part – and you have a case to answer to Nana, His Highness!"

"Oh, I see! Please extend my warmest greetings to Nana and the Village Committee members."

"I will pass it on; now, back to where we left off. We have overwhelmingly decided to take our case to the president of the republic."

"Still, I thought it would have been better to contact the MP first!"

"Hey, my Grandson Frank! Who are you to contradict your Grandpa! Bear in mind that I saw your mother growing up as a little girl in the village, so do not create the impressions of being better informed than your grey-haired Grandpa – and the Village Committee at large."

"All honour, Grandpa!"

"I am calling to request you to use your good contacts to your party hierarchy to secure an appointment with the president without delay. You are going to help us – yes or no?"

13

"I will do my utmost, Grandpa! Please give me a day or two to get back to you. I have a few things to sort out today. I will visit Jubilee House, the presidential palace, first thing tomorrow morning and speak with the chief of staff on the matter. He is a good friend of mine."

"That is reassuring."

"Arranging for my Grandpa to meet the president is not a big issue for me; the only problem is the urgency attached to it. Still, I will do all I can to ensure it happens."

Just as I was about to end the call, it occurred to me I needed to warn him not to reveal my real credentials as he tried to arrange the meeting with the president; I did not want to create the impression I was behind the petition.

"Don't end the call yet", I urged him.

"I thought we were finished?"

"Just a last point; do not reveal my credentials to anyone. If you are asked details about the petitioners, just let them know they are ordinary residents of your little village."

***

Frank called the next day as promised. After the initial greetings, he went straight to business:

"I went personally to the office of the chief of staff to try to secure an appointment. As expected, it was not easy due to the short notice. 'The president is fully booked for the next several weeks – the next free slot is eight weeks away,' I was told.

"Just as I was about to leave the office to report back to you, his phone began to ring. It happened to be from the president's secretary. She revealed that a traditional leader had called to request the postponement of a meeting scheduled for next week. In the end we were offered the slot. It is at 10am next Friday – not tomorrow, but the next.

"So, Grandpa, please pass the message on to the committee. I have spoken with my wife. We will be happy to allow you to sleep over here the night prior to the meeting – to offer you the opportunity to rest and prepare for the meeting."

"I am proud of you, my little politician Grandson! Keep on engaging with the powers that be – who knows, you yourself might ascend to the office of the presidency one day!"

"Well, let's wait and see what the future holds. Grandpa, before we end the conversation, I want to stress that we are able to host you only one night; no more than that!"

"What is going on in Ghana, Frank?"

"What do you mean, Grandpa?"

"I mean, how dare you set a limit on how long your visiting Grandpa is permitted to stay at your home? In former times when I wanted to visit relatives, what mattered was my transportation. The moment I had enough to pay for my journey, I got into a vehicle and embarked on the journey. On my arrival, even though they were not expecting me, I was always welcomed to stay!"

"Well, Grandpa, now Ghana is becoming like Europe."

"You have never been to Europe, so how do you know?"

"Ach, Grandpa, it is the age of the social media! I don't need to travel to Europe to know what is going on there!"

"So, you are copying the European way of life and abandoning the traditional Ghanaian hospitality, eh?"

"Well, Grandpa, in this particular instance, the change in attitude has come about not out of a desire to copy outsiders, but rather owing to the rising cost of living. Though goods abound on the market; they are not affordable for everyone. Everyone is trying their own way to survive. When I am struggling to balance the load on my head, do you expect me to accept someone else's burden?"

"Thanks for your help; one night, after all, is better than none."

"Exactly!"

"If I heard you right, the meeting is scheduled for 10am on that day. Hopefully it will be over in good time to permit us to return to our little village in good time before the fall of darkness. I understand these days it is no longer safe to travel at night in many parts of the country due to the threat of armed robbers. I don't want to die at the hands of a highway robber."

"Hey, Grandpa, I thought having seen many days you are no longer afraid to die!"

"If I have to die, then let it be peacefully, and not on account of the bullets of a bandit!"

***

The three delegates and I met a day prior to our departure to Accra to plan for our trip and devise a strategy to follow during our meeting with the president. After explaining the concept of the welfare state to them, I advised that we make its introduction into the country our cardinal demand to the president.

We will make the president understand we were aware the country was poor so could not afford a generous system as pertains in other parts of the world. Still, we will point out to him that, however limited the resources at the disposal of the state, a start is needed to be made in that direction. More than 60 years after independence, we will stress, the state could not continue to shun her responsibility for its citizens who fall through the social net.

Extended family members who are usually looked upon by other members of the family for help in times of need, we will tell the president, have no legal obligation to cater for the disadvantaged members of society. The state, on the other hand, bore responsibility for the well-being of its citizens. Ghana, after all, was signatory to the UN Human Rights Convention, which guarantees minimum living conditions for all.

To start with, we will call for a minimum payment of 2.50 GHc (approximately $0.50) per day for all who fall below the poverty line. That, in our opinion, is the barest minimum required for one to keep one's head above water financially, considering the prevailing economic situation.

Should the president counter with a statement like "the state coffers are empty, where do we get the money from?!", we would respond by telling him we politely disagree with him. We will at that juncture point out to him that in our opinion considerable savings could be made in the public finances through radical cost-cutting measures. This, we will continue to point out, will involve sweeping cuts in the number of parliamentarians, ministers, presidential staff, etc.

Aware that the limited time at our disposal might not permit us to tell the president everything on our mind, we decided to put our proposals on paper. We would keep a copy for ourselves and present a copy to him for his perusal.

In order not to create the impression we were not as poor as we claimed to be, we decided to dress just the same way we did on an average day.

Just as we thought we had reached consensus on all the matters discussed and were about to depart to our various homes, the only female member of the delegation called everyone to attention, and began:

"I am a lady; I will feel ashamed to appear in casual clothes before his excellency the president."

"No one is saying you should dress inappropriately", Douglas interposed. "We are only saying we should not create the impression of being wealthy and therefore should dress modestly!"

"But you were saying we should dress ourselves the way we do on any ordinary day. I wanted to put on something chic", she smiled. "I wanted to show my pretty self to the president."

"Hey Adwoa, the president is over 70 and married, so you have no chance!" Douglas said, mockingly.

"I am not aiming primarily at the president", she giggled. "Who knows, dressing well might cause one of the presidential staff to take a closer look at me!"

"Well, our mission is to present a petition and not to help others find their partners", Kwootwe joined in the conversation.

"Well, I suggest we grant our princess an exemption, if only for once, and allow her to put on what she deems fit", Douglas pleaded, sarcastically.

"Thanks for your support; as a matter of fact, I was joking. I have nothing extraordinary. I will just put on the clothes I received from 'someone' for Christmas."

"Which 'someone'?" Douglas inquired.

"Hey, Douglas, don't try to poke your nose into someone else's private matter. Or are you trying to eye her?" Kwootwe teased him.

"Of course not! You all bear witness I am happily married with my flower, Comfort."

"I know you are married; whether you are happily married is between you and her!" Kwootwe quipped.

"Okay, just to put the record straight, no one bought anything for me. It was me myself who presented myself something for Christmas?" Adwoa explained.

"How did you manage to earn the money?" Douglas asked.

"Order please!" Kwootwe called out. "As the eldest member of the delegation, I take the privilege upon myself to call an end to the discussion. So, goodnight everyone."

The rest of us sided with him. Agreeing to meet at Kwootwe's home at 11am the next day to embark on our journey, we departed to our various homes.

***

We left home around midday and headed for Accra.

As previously mentioned, Mpintimpi lies about 150 kilometres to the north-west of Accra. We needed to travel first to Nkawkaw, the next main town about 30 kilometres to the north to catch another vehicle that would take us to our final destination.

Not long after we had taken our seats inside a makeshift wooden shed a few metres away from the road that served as a "bus stop" for commuter minibuses, one such vehicle pulled to a stop. Fortunately, it had enough space left for all four of us.

The road we travelled on from Mpintimpi to Nkawkaw displayed gaping potholes, in urgent need of maintenance in many places – not a road a driver unfamiliar with conditions to venture on, especially at night.

As if the driver had memorised the exact location of each of the potholes, he managed to manoeuvre his vehicle around them just in time to avoid hitting them.

The rains had been frequent over the last several days. Whilst worsening the condition of the pot-hole ridden road, it led to the blossoming of the vegetation. Indeed, if the state of the vegetation on each side of the road was anything to go by, the much-talked-about climate change had had little or almost no impact on the ecosystem unfolding before our eyes. Nature seemed, indeed, to be at peace with itself.

It was approaching midday when we got to Nkawkaw. It promised to be a hot day. The midday sun was high in the heavens, the heat scorching. I had a cotton handkerchief; not so the other members of the group. Just as we were looking around for a shop to purchase handkerchiefs, a street hawker, a young lady in her mid-20s who was skilfully balancing on her head a tray packed with various wares, which happily included a few bundles of handkerchiefs, approached us.

"Come over please", Douglas called out to her. "You are really a godsend!" he added as she caught up with us.

"I have been roaming the street the whole morning", she said, beaming with joy. "I have not made any sales so far. Thank God for directing me to you!"

After each team member had chosen a handkerchief, we made our way to the "lorry station" where vehicles waiting for passengers heading for various destinations were lined up. It happened to be about five minutes' walk away. The vehicle at the front of the queue of vehicles heading for Accra was half full when we reached it. It still needed half a dozen passengers to fill it up. About 15 minutes after we had taken our seats, a couple accompanied by a young lad aged about six arrived.

"There is no seat for your son; you need to allow him to sit on one of your laps – are you happy with that?" the driver's mate asked them.

"Not very delighted, but we need to move on", the boy's mother replied.

Moments later we were on our way. I will spare the reader any further details of our journey experiences.

We arrived safely at Frank's accommodation in Madina, a suburb of Accra, at a little after 7pm. After his lovely wife had served us a wonderful dinner, we prepared for and rehearsed what we would say at the important meeting ahead of us.

Frank gave us some tips and advice.

"Though the meeting involves the president", he began, "I want to make you aware of how to address ministers and members of parliament as well, in case we happen to come across some of them in or around the presidential palace. The president may also decide to invite some to be present at the meeting.

"I don't know the situation in other parts of the world. Over here, however, we address our minsters and MPs with the title 'Honourable'. Assuming I were an MP, and you met me on the street, you cannot just call me 'Frank'. Instead, you have to call me 'Honourable Frank', or just 'Honourable'!'"

"Who came up with that idea?" Douglas asked.

"I think we copied it from the English; please correct me, Grandpa, if I am wrong."

"When I wrote to the MP for my area in the UK, I addressed her as "Honourable Mrs..." in the letter. When I met her personally at her office, as far as I remember, she introduced herself with her first name, so I used that name to refer to her throughout the meeting."

"Well, if it was here, you would have had to resort to using 'Honourable' throughout the discourse, otherwise the individual might have felt offended."

"Frank, I know you who are into politics have the inclination not to always say things as they are. But, to be honest, do you think every one of our MPs deserves to be called 'Honourable'?", Douglas asked, mockingly.

"Well, that's a matter for debate; the fact remains, however, that they feel insulted if they are not addressed that way!

"So to recap", Frank continued after a short pause. "MPs and ministers are to be addressed as 'Honourable'. The president, on his part, carries the title 'His Excellency'."

"His Esse – s-s-ensi?" Kwootwe, who never enjoyed the privilege of formal education, struggled with the pronunciation.

"His Excellency!" Frank assisted him.

"His Eessesisi...." Kwootwe wrestled further to get it right.

"No, 'His Excellency'!" Douglas corrected him.

"I don't feel obliged to memorise it! Everyone in the village calls him 'Nana', I will do likewise when I meet him."

"I personally think there is no need to address him with the title 'His Excellency'!" I joined in the discussion. "His name begins with Nana. We are all aware Nana is a royal title in our culture, used for a king, a chief, an elderly person, and so forth. Why on Earth should we put an English title before an indigenous title of honour and respect!?"

21

"I agree with you, Grandpa. We need, however, to keep to protocol! 'When in Rome, do as the Romans do!'

"So please note everyone – for I won't be present to prompt you – after you have been ushered into the presence of the president, you should move forward in a group, and greet him as if with one voice: 'Good morning, Your Excellency, Nana Addo Dankwa Akufo-Addo, President of the Republic of Ghana! We are very honoured and privileged to meet you.'"

At that stage Adwoa directed her gaze at Kwootwe and said mockingly:

"Those who are unable to address him in full are advised to keep their mouths shut!"

"Hey, Adwoa, you have got to show your old man some respect!" said Kwootwe.

"I *am* a respectful young lady, am I not?"

"Well, well, well!"

"That doesn't sound convincing, Old Man!"

"Hey, you guys, do you find me nasty?" Adwoa turned to the rest of the group.

"You are okay, Sister", Douglas replied

"Thanks a lot, Brother."

Having agreed on how to address the president, we went on to rehearse what we would tell him.

3

Free advice for the Ghanaian President on cost saving measures

Our appointment was for 10am. Not wanting to risk turning up late, which, as Frank warned, could result in our appointment being cancelled completely instead of being rescheduled, we left well ahead of time.

Several years ago, traffic in Accra, even during the morning rush hour, was sparse. No longer. A policy of market liberalisation adopted in the country several years before had led to increased commercial activity in the city, which in turn had led to an increase in the volume of traffic.

As we slowly inched our way through the congested traffic, it appeared to me as if the first and the third worlds had collided on the streets of the nation's capital with modern and sophisticated vehicles competing with very old ones, some of which might well be described as death traps more suitable for the scrapyard than the roads.

The two extreme types of vehicle stuck in the traffic might well be symbolic of the economic situation prevailing in the country. Indeed, whereas some were living a lifestyle akin to that prevailing in the first world, others like the delegates I was accompanying to the presidency were struggling to make ends meet.

One could well compare the situation in the country with a pyramid – the few blessed ones sitting on the top whilst the majority, the poor and the destitute, were crushed at the bottom.

As I pondered on the crass inequality in the distribution of wealth in the country, I pictured myself walking in a desert. Before me was a predominantly rugged wasteland, barely endowed with vegetation. As I moved on, however, I occasionally encountered patches of oases boasting blooming green vegetation and springs of crystal-clear water.

Finally, we arrived at the premises of the Golden Jubilee House, which serves both as office and residence of the president. A few days prior to our arrival, on 29 March 2018 to be specific, the previous name, Flagstaff House, had been replaced by the new one.

As we headed for the main gate, Frank gave us a short background history of the premises.

The original Flagstaff House building was constructed in 1845 by the British colonial authorities and served administrative purposes. After the country's independence on 6 March 1957, President Nkrumah, the man who led the country into independence, turned it into the seat of government and presidential residence.

After the military coup that overthrew his regime in February 1966, the seat of government was moved to the Christiansburg Castle. Built by Danish settlers in the 1660s, the imposing castle is situated a few hundred metres away from the shores of the Atlantic Ocean, in the Osu suburb of the capital.

Following extensive renovation in 2015, the Flagstaff House premises once again assumed the role of seat of government and presidential residence.

We followed Frank, who seemed to know every nook and cranny of the area. After walking about 50 metres from the gate, we arrived at the first security checkpoint.

One of the security staff, a young lady of about 25 years who happened to know Frank, turned to him and asked:

"Who are these?"

"This is my Grandpa, this is Kwootwe, this is Adwoa, this is Douglas; they are all from my little village, Mpintimpi", he replied.

"Mpintimpi? Booh! Where is it located?"

"I won't tell you! You go back to school to revise your geography of Ghana!"

"Well, not for the sake of Mpintimpi!" she countered. "By the way, where are you heading for?"

"We have an appointment with the president."

"With the president!?"

"You heard me right."

At that juncture she cast a contemptuous look at the group, singling out Adwoa for particular scrutiny.

"Frank, this is no disrespect to your people; but I was expecting them to dress in a manner befitting the occasion."

Even before Frank could respond, Adwoa, who had been boiling with rage from the rude attitude of the public servant towards them, burst out:

"What do you mean by 'appropriate', Madam?"

"Decent clothing made of Kente or Batik!" she replied, in a mocking tone.

"Mind you, Madam, not everyone in the country is as blessed as yourself to land a well-paid job at the presidency. What we are wearing is exactly what we can afford." Adwoa's reply was stated emphatically.

"No offence was meant, Madam, I am only pointing out what is expected of visitors to the highest office of the country."

"I hope you will bear in mind, Madam", Douglas joined in the conversation. "the fact that he is a president not only of the wealthy, but also the poor. If we are to abide by the dress code you are alluding to, only the well-to-do can have access to the presidency!"

"Please, let us not prolong matters; let us instead leave the matter to rest", Frank urged us.

I thought we had put the security behind us; but, no, we had to go through a few more checkpoints.

Finally, after passing through several doors and walking along several corridors, we came to a large hall that served as the last reception area for visitors to the presidency.

After waiting for about 15 minutes we were asked to follow an escort on the final walk to the presidential office. At that juncture Frank bade us goodbye and headed for his office. The plan was to give him a call after we were done with the president for him to meet us at the gate and drive us to the central bus station, to catch a vehicle to take us back from where we came.

After following a gentleman, whose age I put around 30, for a distance of about 20 metres along a passageway, we finally arrived at the door to the office of the most powerful citizen of the country.

After keying in a security code, the door opened to reveal a spacious office, the walls of which were coloured peach. The room was well cooled, which made me think I was somewhere in Europe rather than in the heat of Africa.

The president was seated on a black leather swivel chair, behind an imposing mahogany desk, which had the emblem of the Republic of Ghana engraved on the front. A prominent flag of Ghana was placed at one corner of the huge wooden desk.

Though I was seeing him for the first time, I recognised him instantly – thanks to the fact that he was one of the most photographed individuals in the country.

Was it because of the age of Kwootwe, was it because of Adwoa's disability? Whatever the reason behind his behaviour, instead of remaining in his seat to greet us, the president stood up and walked towards us the moment we entered the office. After shaking the hands of each one of us in a friendly manner, he bade us take our seats on sofas that had been aptly arranged in a semi-circular manner in one corner of the sizable room. The president took his seat on a brown, luxurious couch facing the group. And so, finally, the ordinary folk of Mpintimpi were privileged to enjoy the company of the Number One citizen of the country.

Nana Addo Dankwa Akuffo-Addo, his was the case of "third time lucky". Having lost two attempts to win the presidency, his party nominated him for what they termed the "third and last attempt". His victory was greeted with frenetic jubilation by his teeming supporters, including, as I was told, the large majority of residents of Mpintimpi. Almost 18 months on, hardly anything had changed in my dear little village of birth. If the general mood of the residents was anything to go by, the initial euphoria had given way to disillusionment.

With his personal secretary taking notes, the president asked us briefly to let him know the reason for our visit.

"Your Excellency, we have been sent by the people of Mpintimpi to congratulate you on your election to the highest office of the country", Douglas began.

"You are welcome", the president responded, a broad smile on his face. "I learnt about your visit a couple of days ago. Just to get an idea of where you are from, I carried out my own inquiry. This is what I found out – you may correct me if I am wrong. Your village is about seven kilometres to the north of Akim Abirem, the capital of the Birim North District of the Eastern Region, right?"

"Yes indeed, your Excellency", replied our spokesperson.

"I recall I visited there a couple of years ago. I was there to attend the funeral of the father of our constituency chairman – in my capacity as the leader of the NPP."

"It was the funeral of Frank's father. He passed away under tragic circumstances. I recall seeing you there", said Douglas.

"For your information, Mr President, Frank is my grandson", I joined in the conversation, before realising we had agreed to allow only Douglas to speak on our behalf!

"Oh, I see", said the president.

"Frank's mother happened to be the daughter of my late brother, the first child of our parents. Mr President is aware of our culture so I need not explain why I refer to him as my grandson rather than great-nephew, not so?"

"Yes, I get it."

After a short silence the president asked:

"How is Frank doing?"

"His usual cheerful and lively self, your Excellency!" Douglas replied.

"We won your constituency in the last election, didn't we?"

"Yes indeed. What else did the main opposition party, the National Democratic Congress [NDC], have to expect in a place where the hearts of the overwhelming majority of the population beat for the NPP!"

"An excellent piece of good news, hurray! We should guard against complacency though. We should rather keep on engaging the electorate, to ensure we maintain the seat for as long as possible. Mind you, the opposition is not asleep."

If he had expected us to continue singing praises to the party for as long as it takes, he would be well advised to be prepared for a less harmonious encounter.

"Sir, with all due respect", Douglas began, "we are disappointed at the present state of affairs in our village"

"Why?" he inquired, clearly taken aback.

"Your Excellency, allow me to use the case of my uncle to make my point. He is over 80 years old. He fought actively for independence by galvanising support for the movement in our village and its surroundings. Since independence he has laboured hard on the land to help sustain his family. Apart from growing food for their own consumption, he also cultivated cocoa.

"It is no secret that the cocoa beans he and other cocoa farmers, like myself, produce, have been and continue to be the main source of much-needed foreign currency for the country.

"Over the years we were promised, among other things, the setting up of a cocoa farmers' pension scheme to take care of us in our old age – but nothing has materialised. Now he is 80 years plus and no longer in a position to work. His cocoa farm was ravaged by fire a while ago. He is receiving help from no state agency. Had it not been for the solidarity of extended family members, he probably would have starved to death by now.

"Mr President, we are hungry. As the saying has it, 'a hungry man is an angry man'. Our anger is not directed specifically against you and your government but against many others that came before your administration. We have suffered patiently for a long time – but no longer. The chief of our village, Nana Kofi Du Ampem IV, in consultation with the Village Committee has sent us to you to lay bare our grievances.

"Mr President, we want to make one thing clear, our mission has nothing to do with party politics, nothing to do with the two main parties in the country, NPP and NDC. We just spoke about the fact that the NPP candidate won in our constituency. Without wanting to name names, I want to stress that the majority of the individuals in our delegation voted for your party.

"I want to reiterate, Mr President, the timing of our action is pure coincidence and has nothing to do with your government *per se*. As a matter of fact, the frustration and anger have built up over the last several years. Having waited in vain for anyone to take care of us, we have decided to bring the matter to your attention.

"Mr President, I have the impression the politicians care little about the common people, indeed the poor and the underprivileged. I presume they take us for stupid and uninformed, so they choose to do what they wish with us. Their attitude, whether from your party or the opposition NDC, is to approach the poor and illiterate folks for their votes when elections are pending; once the elections are over no one hears from them!

"Mr President, the natural resources of this country, be it gold, be it diamonds, be it oil, were created for every citizen of the country. We want to claim our due share of it.

"Nana, much as we accept that the problems we face are not entirely of your making, we would have thought that, on assumption of power, you would make a gesture to the populace if only to create the impression, yes underscore, the fact that you are bent on making savings, earmarking money to spend on projects to help lift the populace out of poverty.

"Judging by the number of ministers you have appointed since assuming power, I have the impression – I may be wrong – that that is not the case."

Was it a pause to gauge the president's reaction? Was it a pause to reflect on what to say next? Whatever the reason, Douglas suddenly stopped speaking, his gaze still fixed on the president.

Clearly taken aback by the frank talk of our spokesperson, the words seemed to have deserted the president who, judging by his appearances on radio, TV and other media outlets, is normally quite chatty.

When nothing seemed to be coming from our prominent host, Douglas went on.

"Mr President, may I at this juncture have your special attention. On behalf of Nana Kofi Du Ampem IV, our honoured traditional leader and the entire population of our little village, I am hereby presenting our cardinal demand to the government of the Republic of Ghana: we are pleading for the creation of a welfare state system in our country in the shortest possible time.

"We presume your Excellency is aware of what such a system entails. We are happy to meet you, Mr President, to discuss further details of our proposals at any place and time of your choosing."

If his facial expression was anything to go by, the president appeared flabbergasted, indeed stunned, by what he was hearing.

"I need to come in here, my friend from Mpintimpi", the president interrupted him. "Did I hear you right – you are calling for the introduction of a welfare state system into Ghana, eh?"

"Yes, your Excellency, you heard me right!"

"You are really sure of what you are talking about?"

"Yes, Mr President!"

"Okay, gentlemen and lady, I am not trying to blow my horn before you; the fact remains that I am well-read on the subject. I want to assure you, I am well informed regarding how the welfare state system operates in a place like the UK. For now, however, let us assume I have no idea of the system, so please explain it to me."

"Mr President, I want to pass the sceptre to a fellow member of the delegation", he said, pointing at me. "He is in a better position to explain the nitty gritty to your understanding." He turned to me. "Kofi", he said, making use of the first name I grew up with in the village, "please explain the matter to the president based on the research you conducted into the theme."

"Mr President", I began, "the welfare state is a concept of government in which the state plays a key role in the protection and promotion of the social and economic well-being of its citizens.

"Under the system, it is the responsibility of the state to cater for those unable to avail themselves of the minimal provisions for a good life. In other words, the state becomes the parent of everyone. As a father is expected to do, the state provides assistance to citizens like Adwoa and my very honoured Old Man who are incapable of caring for themselves, to sustain them.

"The assistance could be in the form of physical cash, coupons that they can exchange for food and other provisions, food they can pick up from food banks, etc.

"We are giving your Excellency nine months to work out the modalities towards the implementation of the policy; otherwise we shall mobilise all the downtrodden of this country on a march to the seat of government.

"Mr President, that in the nutshell is the main demand of the citizens of Mpintimpi on the government. Of course, we are not asking the state to cater for us only, but every citizen of the country who fulfils a set criterion."

If the expression on his face was anything to go by, the president was shell-shocked by the openness, indeed by the bold manner, in which our case was presented.

"I really took you for ordinary peasants from a humble village", the president said. "How did you get to know about the welfare state system?"

"Mr President", Douglas resumed his role, "I am not directing this comment to you specifically. It is meant instead for our politicians in general. Indeed, I do often get the impression you consider us, the ordinary citizens, like a ball in a football game, where you can kick the ball around to serve your whims and caprices. I also have the impression, at times, that you consider us as a kind of spare tyre that you keep in your boot to turn to only in times of need. In a sense, we become important only when elections are pending. At that stage politicians of all parties descend on us to promise heaven on Earth, only to desert us when the elections are over.

"As you can now see for yourself, we are not as illiterate or ignorant as some of you take us to be."

After a short silence, the president made his carefully considered reply. In his cool and collected manner, he began:

"The welfare state system is indeed a really honourable proposition. Whereas I would wish to introduce it into our country, unfortunately our economy is not sound enough to support it. We inherited a huge public debt from the previous government. We are putting measures in place to address the problem. It will be counterproductive to incur further debts through the introduction of such a scheme."

"Well, Mr President, we beg to disagree with you on the matter. I believe with proper management of resources you could find the needed resources to fund the venture."

"I am running the country; I am briefed regularly by the relevant ministers and authorities about the fiscal state of the country, so I know what I am talking about.

"Currently, the population of Ghana is approximately 30 million. Assuming we decide on an average daily payment of 5 Ghc [about 1 US dollar] to the needy and assuming a third of the population qualify for support – which based on the widespread poverty might well be the case – that would amount to 50 million GHc [10 million US dollars] a day! Where on Earth are we going to find the money, eh?"

"Mr President, we are not demanding 5 GHc minimum payment; we could even start with a fraction of that amount, say 2.50 GHc. What is important to us is that the government takes steps to introduce the system without delay. Sixty years have passed since independence. In our opinion, it is high time the state took direct responsibility for the very poor of society rather than leave them at the mercy of extended family members, many of whom may also be struggling to make ends meet. Indeed, we demand action *now*; no kicking of the ball into the unknown future!

"On the matter of funding the venture – we deliberated the matter in detail in our little village before setting out on our journey. In the process we identified several cost-cutting measures that can lead to the saving of huge sums of money that can be spent on the scheme.

"We have written out our cost-cutting measures in a document. We shall leave the president a copy. For now, I will touch briefly upon the salient points:

"To begin with, we are calling for a reduction in the number of our parliamentarians. When, after the military coup of 1966, the military returned the country to civilian rule in 1969, the parliament consisted of 120 members. Today the number has more than doubled to 275 MPs!

"Mr President, the size of the country of Ghana has remained the same since independence. The only thing that has changed is the population. One may argue that an increase in population warrants an increase in the number of parliamentarians. We, the impoverished residents of Mpintimpi, are of a different view.

"It may be the case that some wealthy countries elsewhere have a formula in place that calls for the number of parliamentarians to be based on the size of the population. The fact that a wealthy country somewhere on the globe can afford such a system doesn't mean we should also adopt such a system in our country.

"Though the population has grown, we are still of the opinion that 120 highly competent and highly dedicated MPs – if not even fewer! – are capable of doing the same job. We are therefore calling for a reduction in the number of MPs during the next legislative period. The money so saved will flow into a separately created account to help fund the proposed welfare state system.

"As a next step, we are calling for a radical reduction in the number of ministers of state.

"In this connection, we have decided that in view of our current desolate financial situation, until further notice, the number of ministers in any government present or in future should not exceed 15. As in the case of MPs, it is also our conviction that 15 cabinet ministers, supported by dedicated civil servants, will be able to keep the state apparatus working.

"Next we turn to the matter of deputy ministers. Currently there are two or three deputy ministers per each ministerial position – we are calling for the number to be reduced to one deputy minster per cabinet minister in this and all future administrations.

"As part of our preparation for this meeting, we visited the official website of the government to inform ourselves regarding the makeup of your government.

"Based on the information published there, your present administration is made up of around 120 ministers and deputy ministers. We, the poor and deprived of our little village, cannot stomach such 'bloating' of the size of government.

"We have consequently proposed a cabinet re-shuffle, to reflect our decision to limit the number of minsters and deputy ministers to 15 each. Time will not permit us to go through the list and explain what led us to drop some of your current ministerial appointments whilst merging some of them. We have outlined our reasons in a document that I want at this stage to present to your Excellency."

At this stage Douglas pulled a brown envelope from his pocket and handed it to the presidential secretary.

"I will take my time to go through it myself", the president declared.

"I sincerely hope you will act on our recommendations. As already stated, I am not going to go through the whole list, which would take more time than we have available now. Just to cite only two examples: we unanimously agreed to do away with the portfolios of Senior Minister and Minster for Evaluation. Your Excellency might have had his own reasons for creating those two ministerial positions. We, the poor and deprived residents of Mpintimpi, on our part did not recognise the need for them.

"I am sure other deprived citizens living in the slums of Nima, Kejetia, Agbogbloshie, aka Sodom and Gomorrah, will think the same."

After a short break, Douglas continued:

"Mr President, I heard on the radio recently that your government is considering creating six additional regions to the ten existing ones. Your Excellency, may I please know if that is the case?"

"Indeed, it is; towards that goal I have created a ministerial portfolio, Minster for Re-Regionalisation to oversee the process. The idea of the creation of the additional regions did not originate from me. During my travels through the regions as the leader of the opposition, the traditional leaders I came into contact with kept on pressing for the creation of additional regions for various reasons. You are aware of the tribal diversity of the country. Some of the traditional leaders in some of the regions feel discriminated against by the majority tribes of their respective regions and are demanding separate regions for themselves."

"Mr President, our delegation is against the idea."

"Why?"

"For several reasons, your Excellency. Time will not permit me to dwell on all of them, but I will touch on the two main reasons.

"In the first place, it is our opinion that the size of our country does not warrant 16 regions.

"Added to this is the cost factor. Six additional regions will imply the creation of six additional ministerial positions. Six ministerial positions will call for the creation of at least six additional deputy ministerial positions.

"It is also customary in this country for every minister and deputy minister to be provided with an official vehicle, which in almost all cases involves a Toyota Landcruiser 4x4. That will imply the acquisition of at least 12 additional vehicles of that make to add to the several hundred acquired for ministers and MPs.

"Also, it is customary for the state to offer minsters of state and other high-ranking officials fringe benefits such as free accommodation, free fuel, a chauffeur, a house boy, a garden boy and in some cases even a maid.

"Without doubt, the creation of the six new regions will add an extra burden to an already strained state economy.

"Earlier in our discussions you pointed out that the state does not have the fiscal means to implement our proposed welfare state scheme. No money for the poor and deprived; yet sufficient money for the ruling class.

"With the exception of only a few past leaders, that seems to be the thinking of our leaders, past and present, no matter to which regime they belonged.

"Apart from trimming down the size of government, we have also identified several other areas where savings could be made. These include the areas of defence, diplomatic representations, the civil service, etc.

"We have come up with another paper outlining the additional cost-cutting measures we are proposing. Mr President, here is a copy for your perusal." Saying that, Douglas handed the second envelope he was keeping in his pocket to the president.

"I will take my time to go through this as well. In due time, I will let you know my thoughts on the matter. If need be, I will invite you back to the presidency for further deliberations on your proposals and suggestions."

"We are at the service of our beloved country, Mr President. Day or night; rain or sunshine, whenever you call, we shall do your biding!" Douglas assured him.

"In thunder and lightning as well?" he jested, a broad smile on his face.

"Certainly"

"Jokes aside, I must stress that I am really encouraged by ordinary citizens like yourselves who do not wait for everything to be done for them, but are also ready to take the initiative, indeed to contribute to the national debate – more grease on your elbows!"

A short silence followed to gauge our reaction. We kept silent.

"Much as I appreciate your contribution, I want you to be aware that it is not the number of MPs nor the size of my government that is at the heart of our problems. Indeed, whereas there are, without doubt, internal contributory factors to our economic malaise, I want to draw your attention to the fact that the economic problems and challenges facing the country are not entirely home-made or internally created. There are with certainty several external factors contributing to our malaise. Time will not permit me to delve into the details of the matter. For now, I will touch briefly on some of them:

"My government inherited a huge national debt. Yes, we owe millions of US dollars to foreign states and international financial institutions. Our contractual obligations call on us, on a regular basis, to make instalment payments.

"In the end we spend a good proportion of our earnings not only in repaying the various loans, but also the interest accrued on them."

"May I interrupt you, Sir? Did I hear you right that we are spending a good deal of our earnings on debt servicing?"

"That is exactly the case."

"We, the poor countries, paying interests on loans granted by the wealthy countries? Surely not!"

"That is exactly what is happening, my fellow countrymen from poor Mpintimpi. That indeed is the bitter reality on the ground. We could otherwise have spent the money for the betterment of the country, including the introduction of the welfare state demanded by you. I am by no means cold-hearted; it is indeed my heartfelt desire that every citizen in the country gets the basic necessities needed for a decent existence."

"Why don't you, Mr President, make it clear to the foreign creditors that unfortunately we are not in a position to repay our debt in our current situation. We need to let them know we shall surely meet our obligations one day, but for now we are incapable of doing so. I suggest you go to the countryside and take pictures of people living in abject poverty and send it to our creditors. Pictures have a way of telling stories. I believe when they see images of our malnourished children going about barefooted and in tattered clothes, they will appreciate the extent to which we are impoverished."

"Well, my fellow citizen from little Mpintimpi, I do not think such images will make any difference. Unfortunately, in the real world of politics, economics and financial decisions are based on facts and not on virtues such as compassion, benevolence, mercy, etc.

"Apart from the debt burden", the president went on, "another factor hampering our progress as a nation is the fact that our trading partners in the developed countries do not pay fair prices for our goods. Not only are they not paying fair prices for our products, they also impose tariffs on the goods we export to them, making them expensive and uncompetitive on their markets.

"My government, as well as previous ones, have over the years pleaded with our trading partners in the developed world to change their unfair trade practices towards us – to no avail.

"Let me cite only one example. Ghana is one of the leading producers of cocoa. Indeed, our cocoa is very well sought after internationally. In an ideal world you would expect the foreign countries to help establish factories here to process the raw cocoa into finished products such as chocolate, cocoa drinks, cocoa butter, etc., before exporting them to their respective markets.

"Processing the raw products here has several advantages – it enables us to pay our farmers higher prices for the raw cocoa beans, it helps to create jobs and to boost our foreign exchange earnings.

"We have on several occasions invited them to come over with the required capital, machinery and know-how to establish the needed factories. They have so far turned deaf ears to our pleas. They seem to prefer to purchase the raw cocoa beans cheaply for processing in their respective countries.

"Apart from cocoa, there are several other commodities we export in the raw instead of the processed state due to the reasons I have already touched upon. These include timber, palm oil, various minerals, etc."

"That is very sad indeed", Douglas shook his head with a deep sigh.

"Well, that is the reality on the ground. Of course, I will also want the state to cater for the poor and needy; easier said than done, fellow countrymen."

"Concerning the servicing of our debts, Mr President", Douglas continued, "we should make it clear to them that much as we are happy to meet our debt obligations, the topmost priority is to feed ourselves. If needs be, we have to defer our debt repayment for while."

"Easier said than done. We have to obey international laws and regulations. We cannot just walk away from our duties and obligations, otherwise no one will consider granting any further loans in the future."

"Can you not invite them to send representatives to Mpintimpi to see things for themselves, how we are struggling to make ends meet?" Douglas suggested.

"Well, I will pass your message to their representatives here; I doubt though that anyone will take any notice."

After a short silence, one of the president's assistants entered the office and gave us a sign that our allotted time was over.

"Well, I need to attend another meeting", said the president. "I have taken note of the issues raised. I will have a chat with your constituency MP and see how best we can help resolve them."

"This in no disrespect to your Excellency", said Kwootwe. "In the past we received similar promises and assurances that were not followed up with concrete action. We can only hope that this time the promise is kept."

"Rest assured, Old Man, you have my word – my word is my honour!"

Just as we got to our feet and were about to head for the door, the president turned to the oldest member of our delegation and began:

"Old Man, you and your delegation are not returning to your village today, are you?"

"We have to, your Excellency."

"It is quite a distance; do you think you can make it?"

"Your Excellency, we have no choice, we cannot afford sleeping in a hotel", Kwootwe replied.

"You can spend the night in the State Guest House, if you wish."

"That's great, thanks, Mr President. That is most kind of you. That will enable rest for my bones and regeneration for my strength overnight! At the age of 80, my strength is gradually deserting me."

"You are 80?" the president asked, the surprise written on his face.

"Indeed, do I look younger?"

"I took you for 60!"

"I am 80. Though there are no official records to that effect, the source of my information is credible. There used to reside in our village a teacher who regarded it a duty to record the dates

41

of birth of every child born into the village in a notebook he kept especially for that purpose. My understanding is that he also kept a record of all deaths in the community."

"That is a remarkable example of civic duty to the community by a dutiful citizen. Individuals with a remarkable sense of duty, who grasp the initiative to do what is right without waiting for instructions from above. These indeed are the type of citizens we need in our nation's building efforts."

The president turned to one of his assistants and said: "Mr Awartey, take good care of this old man and his group. Get them decent rooms in the State Guest House to spend the night. Do also get them something decent to eat."

Turning to us, the president posed the question:

"Dear friends from Mpintimpi, you realise after all that the state cares for its citizenry, true or false?"

"Who am I, your Excellency, to contradict you?" smiled Kwootwe.

"Do I intimidate you? We live in a free and liberal democracy; you are free to speak your mind."

"Well, if you want to hear it as it is – I have the feeling you politicians are only interested in our votes – and no more!"

"Old Man, I am happy to discuss the matter further, either here or at your home it Mpintimpi."

"You are welcome to spend a weekend with me."

"I will ask my secretary to arrange it."

"Sure?"

"You have my word!"

With a broad smile on our faces, we parted company with our president.

***

Mr Awartey conducted us to a three-bedroom guest house in the premises of the Presidential Palace. Kwootwe and Adwoa were each assigned a room; Douglas and I shared the third.

We were also served sumptuous meals. The three other delegates went for fufu[3]; on my part I opted for banku[4] and tilapia enriched with okro stew.

"I have not eaten anything so tasty for months!" Douglas remarked as he elatedly swallowed the fufu balls that made their way down his throat.

"You better ask Frank to use his connections to get you a job here!" Adwoa, who had kept quiet most of the time, joined in.

"If it is not too late, I read the other day that there are already almost 1,000 workers in the presidency alone!"

"Almost 1,000!" Adwoa exclaimed.

"Yes, the number was published recently in line with the constitutional demands for them to do so annually." Douglas stated. "If I had known beforehand, I would have raised that issue with the president and suggested a radical reduction in the number as part of our cost-cutting measures."

"Almost 1,000 at the presidency alone! That explains why we saw so many people loitering around the compound, corridors, passageways, etc.!" I joined in the conversation.

---

[3]   A meal popular in Ghana and other West African countries. It is prepared by pounding boiled cassava, yams, or plantains in wooden mortar into a doughlike consistency. **Fufu** is eaten with the fingers. A small ball of it can be dipped into an accompanying soup or sauce and swallowed down the throat—does not require chewing.

[4]   Banku is a Ghanaian dish which is prepared by stirring fermented corn dough in hot water over several minutes into a smooth, whitish consistent form. Banku is served with soup, stew or a pepper sauce with fish.

"Including that lady who was so rude to us! I just could not figure out what role she was playing. She did not take part in the search, she just sat there talking and behaving rudely to us!" Adwoa said.

"What criteria was used to pick such a rude person to sit at the entrance to the presidency?" Kwootwe wondered

"Criteria? It is a matter of who you know!" Douglas replied.

"So, if you don't know anyone at the top, you have virtually no chance of ever enjoying a slice of the national cake, eh?" Adwoa sighed.

"Do not harbour any illusions, my friend", Douglas said, a sense of despair written on his face. "The politicians, no matter which party they belong to, are all the same. They care only for themselves, their family members, friends and acquaintances. Citizens like you and me are irrelevant to them!"

The conversation went on for a while. Finally, Kwootwe took a look at the watch on his wrist and remarked, "It is already past 10pm. I need to retire to bed to rest my bones."

"I'll join you, Old Man, I'm equally exhausted", I yawned.

Everyone present joined in the chorus. Soon we dispersed to our respective rooms. Dog-tired as I was, I was soon lost in sleep.

4

The bold resolve of a humble village to challenge global powers

After breakfast the next day, we bade goodbye to our caretaker and headed back to the village, arriving home late in the night. Early the next day, the chief summoned the committee to his residence to listen to what we had to report.

After hearing our report, the chief began:

"I am really proud of you, for bringing our situation before the highest authority in this country. I am however not happy with the outcome. I have during the course of my long reign heard politicians make vague promises that they failed to act upon. I don't believe their assurances and pledges any longer; now I only believe in tangible commitments – projects in the village that create jobs for the youth, for example."

After a short pause, Nana continued:

"Did you say the president blamed external factors for being part of the problem?"

"Correct", Douglas nodded.

"That is typical of our leaders; instead of confronting the problems facing us, devising solutions to our problems, they divert attention from themselves to external factors."

"Well, he claimed our international trading partners are not offering fair prices for our products, not giving us favourable terms for our credits, not creating favourable conditions for our goods to compete in their market, etc. 'We have tried all we can to get them to change their tactics but to no avail.' he lamented. As we listened to him, he might have thought we did not believe his claims, so he looked us sternly in the eye and said: 'You seem unconvinced with what I am telling you. If that is the case, I suggest you travel to the overseas countries involved and find out the truth from their leaders,' he stated."

"Really! Did he say that?"

"Yes, he did. Of course; he was aware we don't have the means to do so. After all, how does he expect people like you and me to bear the cost of such an undertaking?" Kwootwe's facial expression expressed a degree of resignation. "If I had the means, I would do exactly that. I wouldn't be meeting them to present a petition, but rather invite our old masters to come back and look over the administration of the country!"

"Invite the Europeans back to recolonise us!? Did I hear you right?" Douglas inquired.

"Yes, you did."

"That is outrageous!"

"What is outrageous?"

"The idea of subjecting myself to colonial rule!"

"May I know how old you are, Douglas?"

"45."

"I thought as much. That means you were born in Ghana and so have no idea of how we lived in the Gold Coast. I was a little over 15 years old at the time of independence, so I know how life was in the Gold Coast! We were not independent, but at least everything was available and affordable. Corruption was not as widespread in those days as is the case now. People also respected the law; and today? Forget it!"

"So, you are calling for the return of the Europeans to colonise us, eh?" one of those present asked.

"I am not calling for a return of colonial rule."

"But that is what is implied when you call for the return of the Europeans? Isn't it?" Douglas insisted.

"No, you have misunderstood me. We shall maintain our president, our parliament, our ministers, etc. The foreigners could be employed as administrators, special advisors, technical assistants, etc."

"Well, I do not share your view", Douglas protested. "The moment you let them in, it will be very difficult to get them out. I agree with you though on the matter of taking our case to the foreign powers. Indeed, if I had the chance, I would want to meet them to talk face-to-face on some issues of concern to me.

"I left my good position in Accra to come to the village to engage in farming. I have managed, with hard work and dedication, to cultivate a few acres of cocoa. I have over the years watched helplessly as income from the cocoa beans continued to fall.

"So far we export almost every cocoa bean we produce raw to the industrialised countries. I ask myself, why don't those we are exporting to come over here and set up factories to produce the end products and ship them back to their countries? Apart from creating jobs, such a step, I believe, would lead to high prices for the cocoa beans I produce with my sweat and blood.

"At least in that respect", Douglas concluded, "I do share the view of the president that part of our woes is due to external factors."

The exchange went on for a while, speaker after speaker expressing anger mixed with frustration at their dismal economic situation and the fact that no one seemed to care for them.

Eventually, the traditional leader dismissed the meeting.

As I left the meeting, I began to consider the idea of sending a delegation from the village to meet world leaders as first mooted by the president. The head of state, no doubt, had mere sarcasm in mind when he uttered those words.

47

The idea, while sounding adventurous, could possibly impact positively on the cause we were campaigning for.

The story of a group of impoverished peasants travelling all the way from their village in Africa to petition world leaders the likes of Angela Merkel, Theresa May, Donald Trump, etc., might catch the attention of the world press and help spread the message around the globe. Soon the matter might be picked up by groups like human right activists, environmentalists, anti-capitalists, etc., who could join in the campaign and exert pressure on world leaders and force them to change their unfair practices towards the developing world.

The issue that needed to be addressed was money. How could we come by the money needed for such a venture?

It is superfluous to mention here that there was nothing the chief and the village at large could contribute to the undertaking.

I could raise the money needed, though. That would however imply having to stretch my resources, indeed having to withdraw savings I was holding for the future.

Then there was also the issue of cost effectiveness. Wouldn't it be more advantageous to the local population if I invested the money I would spend on the venture in potentially profitable undertakings such as crop and poultry farming?

I wrestled with the matter for the rest of the evening.

Even as I retired to bed, the matter would not leave me in peace, keeping me awake for a while. After turning and tossing in bed for a considerable period – my thoughts occupied the whole time with the pros and cons of sending a delegation from the village to meet world leaders – I was finally overcome by sleep.

On waking up the next morning, I decided, despite some degree of reservation, to finance the overseas mission!

I called on Nana that evening to make my intentions known to him.

"Nana", I began after the initial exchange of greetings, "as we informed you and the Village Committee during our meeting with the president, he lay part of the blame for our predicament at the doors of foreign powers. He urged us to bring our case to them if we so wished.

"Nana, I need not tell you that ruling governments past and present have neglected the village. I don't think the situation will change in the foreseeable future.

"I suggest therefore that we take our case to world leaders, make *them* aware of our predicament. Even if we do not receive help from them directly, a report on our visit in the media could lead others to come to our aid. There are indeed a growing number of influential individuals who have come to the realisation that the world economic system is not treating people like us fairly. Who knows, if our campaign leads one of two of such personalities to come to our aid..."

"Much as I agree with you on the matter", Nana said, "the question that has just sprung to mind is: just how are we going to finance such a trip? You remember how we struggled to find the means to travel to Accra? Indeed, without your assistance that could not happen. If we had to struggle to raise the means to travel to Accra, how do you expect us to find the means to finance the overseas trip?

"I have a surprise for Nana. I am prepared to do that!"

"Really?"

"Yes, for sure."

"I can't believe my ears!"

"Trust me, Nana, I will do what I have promised."

"How many delegates can you sponsor?"

"A maximum of three."

"The saying has it that one should never change a winning team. You can go with the same individuals who accompanied you to the president."

"Indeed, I was about to suggest you select the same individuals who accompanied me to see the president."

"That is not a bad idea!"

"Do I have your go-ahead to summon the Village Committee to inform them about the matter?"

"Indeed, you do!"

The Village Committee met the next day as proposed. Speaking through the *Okyeame*, the traditional leader made known to the gathering the reason for the meeting.

"A delegation from Mpintimpi heading for England to meet Queen Elizabeth, my beloved queen!" Kwaasuo, generally regarded by the rest of the community as one who had gone bananas, burst out in uncontrolled laughter on hearing what Nana had to report. Owing to his impaired mental health he was usually not invited to such meetings. Having got word of the meeting through the announcement of the 'gong-gong' beater he nevertheless decided to turn up all the same.

"No one has the intention of sending a delegation to the Queen of England; we are only planning on sending representatives to meet world leaders", he was told.

"But I thought the Queen is the leader of the whole of *Aburokyire*! [the Western World!]"

"Who told you so?" someone in the hall shouted.

"I used to work as a houseboy in the home of a European couple in Accra. They told me that when I served as a houseboy during my time in Accra! They told me that the Queen is head of *Aburokyire*!"

"Well, that is not true!"

"Who told you that is not true? You have to go back to school to refresh your general knowledge!" he roared.

That was Kwaasuo in his element. A World War II veteran, everyone in the community took him to be crazy. He on his part considered everyone else an idiot, apart from himself and the traditional leader.

"Nana", a dissenter said, "let us not attempt to bite off more than we can chew. Sending a delegation to meet the president was in itself a bold decision. Now we are talking of sending representatives abroad to meet world leaders! When at all will this little community learn to cut its coat according to the size of its cloth?"

Another dissenter added, enraged: "We struggle from morning till evening to feed our children; now we are considering sending a delegation to *Aburokyire*! Why not spend the money on feeding ourselves rather than make a big show to the whole world!"

The discussion went on for a while, with opinions on the pros and cons of the planned trip remaining almost equally split between the two sides.

Finally, Nana, who was the ultimate authority in any matter pertaining to the village, gave a decisive reply. "Thank you very much for your contribution", he said. "I have taken your opinions into consideration. My only issue is how to find someone to finance the venture. Since that is no longer an issue, I will give my green light for it to go ahead. Doc has told me he is able to sponsor a maximum of three delegates. I am suggesting we send the same team that met the president."

On hearing this Kwootwe got slowly to his feet and began:

"Nana, with all due respect! Much as I appreciate the honour accorded me, I doubt whether I have the needed strength for the trip."

"Why not?"

"I have never been to *Aburokyire*. I have heard the place is very cold, as cold as the inside of a deep freezer. How do you, Nana, expect a frail old man like me to survive in such a terrible climate?"

"Well, I have also not been there, so let us hear what Doc has to say to that."

"Nana, Kwootwe is right", I began. "It can be very cold in winter. If everything goes well, we shall be embarking on the journey at the end of April or beginning of May. The weather is generally mild in May so he should be alright. In any case, I will supply them with clothes to keep them warm.

"It will indeed help our cause if he comes along. A frail-looking elderly person, appearing before the powerful men and women of the world to make a passionate appeal to them to take the needs of impoverished peasants from a small African community into consideration in their decision making, will likely call forth their sympathy."

"Yet another issue" – that was Kwootwe again! "As far as I can remember, I have never missed my daily evening meal of fufu in my life. I hear fufu is not available in *Aburokyire*. I am told over there the main meal of the residents is bread spread with either margarine or soft cheese plus tea."

"Who told you so?" someone in the group inquired.

"A friend of mine used to be the houseboy of an English couple in Kumasi. He told me they ate bread and cheese and drank tea every blessed day!"

"Well, I can let you know you won't miss your fufu during the trip", I said assuredly.

"You mean fufu pounded in a wooden mortar with the help of a wooden pestle?"

"I have never come across anyone pounding fufu in *Aburokyire*! No, you won't get pounded fufu. You will however be served fufu prepared by stirring powdered mehl and potato flakes."

"Fufu made through stirring and not pounding! Yuck! That is not for me!"

"Come on Kwootwe, you are only going to spend a maximum of four weeks there. You will definitely survive without the type of fufu you are familiar with", someone in the group sought to assure him.

"Well, whilst still harbouring my reservations, I cannot disobey Nana's instructions, so I will go as instructed. If I die, I die!"

"Ahem, can I make a suggestion? If he dies, just bury him wherever you find space. That will save his family burial costs!" Guess who said that? Kwaasuo!

"If you are praying for me to die in order to pounce on my property, then you are going to wait a long, long time!" Kwootwe hit back.

"What property do you have apart from your tattered clothes!" Kwaasuo retorted.

"Ugh, I can't stand it any longer. We are in the presence of Nana. We are here to discuss serious matters. Everyone has a duty to comport the group!" the *Okyeame* roared.

After the intervention of the traditional spokesperson of the chief, order returned to the meeting. In the end, the group formally endorsed the plan to send Kwootwe, Douglas and Adwoa on the mission to present their petition to world leaders.

***

Having settled the issue of finance and the make-up of the delegation, the group began the necessary preparation for the overseas trip. Apart from me, none of the members of the team boasted a passport. We needed to take the necessary steps to resolve the issue without delay.

From time immemorial it had been difficult for residents of the country to acquire the important travel document. Though I learnt the process had become easier compared to the time I acquired my first Ghana passport over 40 years ago, I am told it is still quite a struggle. In my case, a member of my church used her good contact to the director general of the passport office to help me acquire the important travel document. I doubt if my effort alone would have led to success.

As in the case of our meeting with the president, I decided to seek the assistance of Frank. If he could arrange for us to meet the president at such short notice, he may well be in a position to help us obtain the travel document.

Without much ado, I picked up the phone and dialled his number.

"No problem, I have good contacts with the passport office", he assured me. "If we had known beforehand, we could have applied during your visit", he said. "As it happens, you will now all have to come back to Accra."

"Is it not enough for us to send one person to sort out the matter on our behalf?"

"No, Grandpa. We now have biometric passports, so the applicants have to report in person to have their biometrics taken."

Without further ado, we made arrangements to return to Accra. As on the previous occasion, Frank offered to host us for a night.

Two days later we made our way to Accra. After spending the night with his family, we were conducted by Frank to the passport office. After presenting our documents, we were told to expect our passports in a week or two. We set out on our return journey around midday, arriving at our destination shortly after the onset of darkness.

***

Even as we awaited the arrival of the passports, it dawned on us that without an official Ghana government recommendation letter, it would be almost impossible for people of our calibre and background to get the embassies of the countries we were planning to visit to issue us with visas.

We also reasoned that an official Ghana government recommendation letter would improve the chances of our request for meetings with the world leaders we were intent on visiting being granted.

Yet again, it was Frank who came to mind. I called him to raise the issue with him.

"Just leave the matter with me, I will do what I can to help", he said on hearing the reason for the call. "As I mentioned on a previous occasion, I have very good contacts with the chief of staff. I will plead with him to issue two letters – one for the visa application, the other to help you obtain audiences with the world leaders you intend to meet."

"When should I call for an update?"

"I will come back to you as soon as there is a new development on the matter."

"Okay, I will expect your call!"

That evening just as I had finished my supper, my phone began to ring. I recognised from the number displayed on the screen who was on the line – Frank!

"Good news, Grandpa!" he began after the initial greeting. "The chief of staff has agreed to provide the two letters you require. They should be ready in about a week's time."

"That is very reassuring; thanks for your help!"

"I suggest I keep the letters until the passports are ready. The moment I get hold of the travel documents, I will call you to come over so I can accompany you to the various embassies for the visas."

About a week following the above conversation, Frank sent a text message to confirm receipt of the two letters. A few days later he informed us the passports had been delivered to his address.

The following day we headed for Accra not only to apply for visas, but simultaneously to request the representatives of the Western leaders we intended on visiting to help us secure audiences with their respective leaders.

As on the two previous occasions, Frank promised to offer us accommodation for the night. We reached Accra safely. After supper we rehearsed what we would say when we got to the embassy.

The main reason for our trip was to meet the world leaders involved in person to draw their attention to the pathetic plight of the poor residents of our village in particular, and the poor and deprived of the country at large.

Should the visa authorities suggest we submit our petition to their respective representatives in Accra, we would insist we preferred a face-to-face meeting.

Should any of the embassies demand we let them know our itinerary for the planned overseas mission, we would present it as follows:

Our first place of call will be Berlin for a meeting with the German chancellor, Mrs Angela Merkel. From Berlin we will head for Brussels to meet the president of the European Commission, before moving on to London to meet the British PM Theresa May.

After meeting the named European leaders, we would cross the Atlantic and head for the US. Our first point of call would be the White House for a meeting with President Trump.

We would end our campaign with a visit to the UN headquarters in New York, for a meeting with the UN secretary general. In all we reckoned we would be away for about four weeks.

***

On a bright morning at the end of April, accompanied by Frank, we left for our first visa appointment, which involved the UK High Commission.

The covering letter coming directly from the presidency resulted in the visas being issued promptly. Apart from introducing us, the letter went further to state that, though not being sent directly by the Ghana government, the state would be prepared to pay for our repatriation back home should we, for whatever reason, become stranded.

From the UK High Commission we headed for the German Embassy.

On producing the presidential letter our visas were granted after a short interview. The visas for Germany were also valid for Belgium in line with the Schengen Agreement that abolished border checks between the two countries and other signatory countries.

Our appointment with the US embassy being two days away, we took the opportunity to visit places of interest in the city.

As in the case of both the UK and German visas, we obtained the US visas without much difficulty. An appointment at the White House with President Trump was also confirmed. All was thus set for our overseas mission.

***

Two days prior to our departure, Nana asked the whole village to assemble in a large space in front of his residence, used for community meetings, to bid us farewell.

At a previous meeting of the Village Committee it had been decided to keep the MP for the area in the dark concerning our venture. Having been in that position for almost six years, he had made no impact on the community – so why keep him in the know about a move we had initiated aimed at improving our situation; this was in answer to a question someone asked during the meeting. In the end, the majority of committee members voted to keep him in the dark. Nevertheless, he managed to get wind of the proposed mission. If only for the purpose of staying in a good light with his electorate, he wrote a letter to wish us all the best in our endeavour. The letter was read in the hearing of all at the meeting.

On the day of our departure from the village all and sundry gathered around the commuter stop referred to earlier to bid us goodbye.

The flight the next day was a night flight; departure was around 11pm. We could theoretically have made it to the airport from Mpintimpi. To avoid possible mishaps, we begged and once more obtained Frank's permission to spend the night before the flight at his home.

I will spare the reader the details of the journey from Mpintimpi to Accra.

***

As I lay in bed that night, I pondered the impending trip. I did not expect Douglas, who was quite well educated, to present much, if any, difficulty.

The situation was different with the other two members of the team. Kwootwe, who had received no formal education, had spent most of his life in the village. Beside his limited knowledge of things of this world, he was plagued with ongoing pain from arthritis of both knees. He told me when he last managed to seek medical help several months before, the doctors had recommended X-ray and MRI scans. For financial reasons, he failed to turn up for the examination. Occasionally, when the pain became unbearable, he sent one of his grandchildren to a small shop in

the village to purchase as many paracetamol tablets as his meagre resources would permit.

To facilitate his movement during the journey, I acquired an
elbow crutch for him. I also purchased a stock of simple pain
killers that would last him during the tour.

Then there was the case of Adwoa, who, as already mentioned, was paralysed in the left leg. She manged to attend school
up to primary 6. Though she would have wished to pursue her
education further, that would have meant her having to walk to
the next big village, Nyafoman, to attend the junior high school
there, since there was no such school at Mpintimpi. Her limited
education, coupled with the fact that she had spent almost all her
life in the little village, meant she had only limited knowledge of
life outside of the village.

Concerning her movement, though she was able, with the
help of her crutch, to keep mobile, she could do so only at a
snail's pace.

As if the challenges posed by Adwoa's disability were not
enough, she had made a name for herself in the village for her
unpredictable temperament! She could be calm and collected
one moment, only to burst into fits of anger the next.

***

Right from the outset at Accra International Airport, we got
a taste of what awaited us. On presenting her passport at the
check-in, the attendant looked at her and inquired:

"Where are you heading, Madam?

"London!"

"I thought it is cold there; I don't think you are suita-
bly dressed!"

"Madam, just do what you are employed to do; namely to
check passports!" she burst out. "I am not naked, am I?"

"I did not say that; I am only concerned about your well-being. Having lived in Europe myself, it just came to me instinc-
tively to warn you about your light outfit."

"I don't think it is your business; if I freeze to death, is that
your problem?"

"Adwoa, don't feel offended", I tried to calm her. "She is
only doing her job?"

"I wouldn't have been bothered if she had put the question in
a more friendly manner. But no, she did so in what I think was
an arrogant manner!" She added: "Or maybe she is jealous of
me. That I am heading for Europe whilst she stays back in the
African heat!"

Happily, the check-in clerk kept calm, which helped to de-es-
calate the situation.

"My goodness, this trip is going to be a really tough call", I
murmured to myself.

Happily, the rest of the check-in procedure went without
any incident.

After spending about half an hour in the departure lounge,
we were asked to proceed to our boarding gate.

Just as we were about to join the long queue of passengers,
two airport attendants, each pushing a wheelchair, approached us.

"We have come to assist you to board the plane. As passengers with reduced mobility, you deserve special attention. We
were not aware of that at the outset, or we would have taken care
of you straight away!"

"That is what your colleague at the check-in counter should
have done on seeing me, instead of concentrating on my clothing", Adwoa pronounced. "It should have been obvious that
my uncle and I are vulnerable passengers who need special
attention."

"Apologies, Madam. As the saying goes, it is better late than
never. We will surely take good care of you."

"Okay; please bear in mind though that we are travelling in a group. Without my highly regarded uncle we will not find our way in Europe." She pointed in my direction. "So please make sure you don't separate us!"

"No worries, the flight will not take off until every passenger is on board."

Adwoa and Kwootwe were helped on the plane well ahead of Douglas and I. Eventually we joined them.

Though Douglas and I were assigned adjacent seats and Kwootwe and Akosua to others, we decided to alter the seating arrangement. In the end I sat beside Adwoa, while Douglas sat next to Kwootwe.

5

A clash of two worlds

Finally, the huge aircraft was set in motion. After taxiing on the runway for a while, the colossal man-made bird lifted up into the dark tropical skies.

I took a look through the window. Spread beneath us, and illuminated with innumerable spots of light, was Accra, the city that prides itself as being the place where the first African country south of the Sahara declared independence. The historic event took place over 60 years before, at midnight on 6 March 1957. Has independence fulfilled the expectation of the common man and woman on the street? If the mission we were undertaking was anything to go by, that seemed not to have been the case.

I took a look around to gauge the reaction of the three first-time fliers around me. Apart from Douglas who appeared relaxed, the tension in the faces of the other two was clearly evident.

After the plane had put the take-off and climbing phases of the flight behind us and we were comfortably cruising at great heights above the ground, I turned to have a look at Adwoa. To my surprise she was fast asleep!

Soon she began to snore, not in a mildly audible manner, but in a really stentorian way. Her snoring could be heard not only by those around her, but also by those quite far from us. One gentleman who sat a few rows in front of me turned to me and gesticulated that I should awaken her by means of shaking.

I signalled back that it would be wiser to allow her to sleep for a while.

To my relief and that of the other passengers in the neighbourhood, a cabin crew member came around to serve us. I touched her gently to awaken her, though to no effect.

"Rice or pasta?" the flight attendant inquired. I opted for rice.

"What about the lady?"

I ventured to give her shoulder a shake, applying moderate force – which helped awaken her.

"Rice or pasta?" the attendant inquired.

Still half-awake she muttered something which sounded like "asta".

Thinking she had requested pasta, the stewardess served her the requested meal.

Adwoa thanked her and carefully peeled off the layer of shiny aluminium foil covering her meal package to expose the content.

"Ugh, what is this?"

"Don't you like it?"

"Aw, I thought it was rice."

"The gentleman offered you either rice or pasta; you opted for 'asta'. You've got what you asked for!"

"Oops! I was half-awake. I just responded to the sound of 'astsa' without knowing exactly what it was all about."

"It is pasta covered by a smooth sauce and parmesan; it tastes delicious – try it, you will enjoy it!"

"Not familiar", she pulled a face.

You can have my rice in exchange if you so wish."

"Hmm, I am not sure I like it, still I will give it a try."

Reluctantly she took hold of the plastic fork provided, and with it began to consume the pasta meal.

Was it because of the unfamiliar meal, or was it because of the strange feeling of flying for the first time? Whatever the

reason, the fact remains that shortly after she had eaten a por-
tion of the meal, she began to complain of feeling like vomiting. Moments later she also began to complain of dizziness. "I
have the feeling that everything is spinning before my eyes",
she complained.

Even as I thought of what to say to assure her, it all began –
chunks of food covered in creamy chyme were propelled into the
air, splattering her and my body as well as the back of the seat
directly in front of her and the immediate surroundings!

"Adwoa, what is *wrong* with you?" Douglas, who had taken
note of what was happening, inquired.

Kwootwe who had be awakened from his sleep by the com-
motion around him, turned in our direction and muttered, half
asleep: "All will be well, all will be well." Soon he was lost
again in sleep.

Meanwhile a cabin crew member who happened to be only a
few rows away arrived at the scene.

"Are you alright, Madam?"

Adwoa nodded.

"Please take good care of her whilst I go fetch something to
clean up."

Meanwhile my female compatriot kept on retching, from
time to time vomiting out little amounts of clear liquid into a
plastic bag provided by the flight attendant. The stench of vomit
filled my nostrils.

The crew member returned in no time. She handed me
a towel. As I went about cleaning myself, she helped Adwoa
do the same.

Instead of getting better, she seemed to get worse. Though
the vomiting had ceased, she now complained of a racing heart.

At that stage the flight attendants decided to help her to the
first-class section so she could lie on one of the empty seats. I

asked the other two members of the group to stay behind as I accompanied our unwell compatriot.

"Any doctor on board?" one of the flight attendants announced. "Please report to any of the cabin crew. Your help is urgently needed."

Soon a decently dressed middle-aged man of European descent in a neat black suit and wearing a pair of spectacles got up from several seats ahead of us. Just as Adwoa was given a place to rest, the elegant-looking gentleman caught up with us. Turning to the cabin crew, he began:

"May I please introduce myself. I am Professor Richard Grey, consultant cardiologist at the Queen's Hospital, London. I attended a conference in Accra; I am now just returning home.

"How are you feeling, Madam?" he turned to Adwoa

"Getting better", I said, translating what Adwoa had told me.

The clearly concerned medical officer instructed the cabin crew: "Please check her blood pressure, pulse, blood sugar and temperature."

His instructions were executed in no time. Moments later, a crew member handed him a sheet bearing the results of the tests.

"Her BP and blood sugar are fine; she is also apyrexial – I mean, she hasn't developed a fever; she is also breathing normally. The only issue of concern is her pulse – her heart is beating quite fast. I guess it is more a result of excitement than an organic cause."

"Carry on the flight or consider an emergency landing?" A crew member who had earlier introduced herself as the team leader, inquired from the learned doctor.

"I would suggest we carry on. We only need someone to check on her from time to time."

I sat beside her as the others dispersed. Fortunately, nothing untoward happened to her. About an hour after it all began, she had gathered enough strength to crack some jokes.

"Hey, assuming I had passed away, what would have happened to my body?"

"What do you think?"

"No idea."

"They probably would have opened the window and thrown you into the open space! You have always talked of going to rest in the heavens above one day. The journey to your cherished destination would have been shortened by several thousand metres!"

"Ooh-la-la! I would have grasped your coat and taken you with me!"

After being in the air for about six hours the plane landed safely at Heathrow Airport. A look at the watch on my wrist revealed it was just past 7:30am local time.

After waiting in the transit hall for several minutes, we were asked to proceed to board our connecting flight. It was around midday when we touched down in Berlin.

On noticing the condition of the two other members of the group, we were accorded preferential treatment at the arrival desk.

Soon we were out of the arrival building. We took a taxi and headed for our hotel.

I had opted for an hotel, even though I was aware that my good friend Emmanuel, also a native of Ghana, and his German wife, Anna, who were both of immense help to me when I first arrived in Berlin several years before, would have willingly opened their home to us. I decided against the idea of staying with them on the grounds that I would have felt obliged to reveal to them the reasons for our stay in Berlin. What would have been their take on the venture? Would they have thought their old pal had probably gone bananas by thinking a petition by a delegation of a few simple peasants from an unknown hamlet on the surface of the Earth would have any influence on the mighty men and women at the helm of the affairs of our imperfect world?

We arrived on a Tuesday, and our appointment was scheduled for 10am on the Thursday.

After breakfast the next day, I decided to take them on a sight-seeing tour of the city.

We decided to act and behave exactly the way we do on the streets of Mpintimpi. The only thing that would cause us to act differently would be the weather. Indeed, so long as the weather permitted, we would put on our traditional clothes.

Adwoa came up with an idea I knew would put the other members of the group in an awkward situation, and none of us could convince her to abandon it.

"You are all aware that, despite my disability, I manage to carry items on my head. I am going to do exactly so when we go out shopping. I will put the shopping basket on my head and walk on the street in the manner I am used to doing in the village."

"No please!" I pleaded. "I have been here long enough to be familiar with the mentality of the residents. Already many of them have the perception that the rights of women are not respected in Africa. That perception will surely be verified should they see Douglas and I walking alongside you, with your bag on your head!"

"Still, I want to carry out the 'experiment' to gauge the reaction of the community." She was adamant.

As we stepped onto the street Adwoa, moving slowly holding on to her crutch in one hand, the other hand supporting the shopping bag on her head, caused all eyes to be directed at us.

The sight of Douglas and I walking beside her, apparently unconcerned, was met with consternation by those who passed by.

Soon an elegantly dressed lady aged about 60 approached us.

"Excuse me, don't you have money for a taxi? I am happy to help you out."

"No, we are fine", we stated emphatically, as if with one voice.

"But the lady is struggling, gentlemen. At least the two strong gentlemen should consider helping her."

"Thanks for your concern, Madam. I am fine", Adwoa said, assuredly.

"You may be fine, but the gentlemen are just walking leisurely beside you – I thought they would at least consider it a duty to help you."

"I am fine."

"I am concerned for your well-being. How can you carry that on your head whilst at the same time supporting yourself on a crutch!"

"Please, thanks; that's the manner I have lived in my village since I was big enough to remember."

"Where?"

"In my little village, Mpintimpi."

"Where is that?"

"In Africa; Ghana, to be precise."

"But Madam, we are not in Ghana; we are on the streets of Berlin."

Did the concerned woman call the police to check on Adwoa? We cannot say for sure, but about five minutes after we had parted company with the stranger, a police car occupied by two officers pulled to a halt near us.

"Are you okay?" one of them, a female officer in her mid-20s, inquired, her gaze directed at Adwoa.

"Yes indeed!" Adwoa replied.

"Anything we can do to help?"

"No thanks."

"Gentlemen", the officer turned to us. "The lady is obviously struggling. Why don't you give her a hand?"

"They have offered to help, but I have turned down their offer", Adwoa declared.

"Why?"

"I don't need their help. This is exactly how I go about my life in my village. Should I behave in a different way just because I am in Europe?"

"How are you able to bear your crutch and at the same time balance this bag on your head?"

"Well, that is exactly how I go about my life in my little village in Africa."

"That must be a really harsh life."

"Well, it is not easy; but I have become accustomed to it."

"Well, we just wanted to make sure no one is forcing you into anything that is against your will." She cast a disapproving look at the men in the group as she spoke. "Since that does not seem to be the case, we shall leave you in peace. Please accept our apologies for any distress caused."

I decided to take the group to the foremost shop in the city, Kaufhaus des Westens. Usually abbreviated to KaDeWe, it is reputed to be the second largest of its kind in the whole of Europe.

As we stepped into the halls of the huge department store, I could sense the awe and disbelief in the eyes of the three other members of the delegation.

"Wow! These people seem to be living in paradise!"

"Well, there is an abundance of goods of all kinds here", I acknowledged. "It is far from paradise though."

"What do you mean by that?"

"Well, when I first arrived here, I thought like yourselves that life here is rosy, indeed that because of the material abundance everyone is happy and satisfied with their lives. But the reality is that, despite the abundance of material goods, citizens here are not spared the ups and downs of life."

From KaDeWe, we headed towards the nearest underground station.

"I am taking you to board the underground train", I told them as we went.

"Underground train, really?" Douglas wondered

"Yes indeed."

"Trains travelling under the surface of the Earth! How can that be?" Adwoa asked, sceptically.

"You just follow me. When I first heard about the underground trains I, too, could not imagine how that could be true until I saw things for myself. It is a stark testimony to human engineering ingenuity."

When we got to the station, we were told the lift had broken down. The escalator was working though. Taking into consideration the two vulnerable members in the group, initially I thought of abandoning the idea of taking them downstairs. Seeing the disappointment written on their faces, I decided to venture onto the escalator. I would support Adwoa on the moving staircase whilst Douglas did the same with Kwootwe.

Before venturing onto the power-driven, continuously moving, stairway, I called everyone's attention and began:

"Please be warned – stand still and hold on firmly to the sides of the stairway. Douglas, your duty is to support Kwootwe; I will take care of Adwoa."

"I will manage on my own", she retaliated, radiating a sense of self-confidence.

Instead of standing still and holding firm to the sides as advised, she decided to follow the example of the person just ahead of her and attempted to take a step down the moving stairway! As she did so she lost her balance, stumbled and fell on the moving stairway. My heart leaped within me on beholding the scene.

I bent forward to grasp her before she could roll further downwards. A middle-aged man ahead of her did the same.

71

Fortunately, we managed to hold firmly onto her until we got to the end of the staircase.

"That was scary!" she confessed as she stepped on solid ground.

As we waited on the platform for our train, Kwootwe, clearly taken aback by the underground system, turned to me and began:

"Tell me, how did they manage to dig so deep beneath the surface of the Earth to build tunnels through which trains are capable of travelling?"

"Well, these days they rely on machinery to build such tunnels. In the past they relied mainly on manpower."

"Wow, that must have resulted in the shedding of a great deal of sweat by the workers involved!"

As a magnificent train pulled to a stop at the station, I could see in the eyes of our visitors how fascinated they were by the events unfolding before their eyes.

"Ach! How long and how magnificent they are!" Adwoa exclaimed.

"And the insides – so neat and orderly", said Douglas

"Wow, they seem to be living on a different planet!" Kwootwe joined in the admiration chorus.

As the train sped through the underground tunnels, gliding majestically along the rails, the surprise in the eyes of the visitors from little Mpintimpi was conspicuous.

About 20 minutes after boarding the train, we needed to change trains. The fact that we could do so deep below the surface of the Earth impressed the three even further.

Shortly after emerging from the underground into the busy streets of the German capital, Adwoa, bewildered, turned to me and asked, jokingly:

"Is it possible, Doc, to arrange for me to remain here indefinitely?"

"Tut, tut, we are all heading back to Mpintimpi at the end of our mission!" I declared.

I was keen to take them to places of interest and also show them some of the places in the city that endeared my heart to Berlin during my stay when the city was still divided in the early 1980s.

Realising the slow pace at which Adwoa and Kwootwe were moving, I decided to hire a vehicle for the tour.

I took them to the hostel on the Shoneberger Ufer, where I stayed when I first arrived in the then West Berlin in May 1982. Our next place of call was the Oskar Helene Heim, the orthopaedic clinic where I spent almost five months after undergoing major surgery to my left ankle.

From there we drove to the Wall Museum at Checkpoint Charlie, on the Friedrichstraße 43–45. During the period of the cold war, it was one of the three border crossings of the divided city under the control of the US authority in the city.

I also took them to view a small section of the original Berlin Wall that has been left standing at a spot not far from the Checkpoint Charlie Museum to serve as a reminder of the cold war days.

As I stood before the small remnant of the wall, my thoughts went back to the time I resided in West Berlin, between 1980 and 1982. How could I at that period in time ever have imagined that the wall would crumble in the not distant future and lead eventually to German reunification?

After spending several hours sight-seeing, we returned to our accommodation very exhausted indeed.

As in the case of our visit to our president, we spent the evening prior to our meeting with the German chancellor rehearsing what we would say. I shall spare the reader the details, apart from revealing that, as in the case of our visit to Jubilee House, we appointed Douglas as our spokesperson. I decided as before that I would keep a low profile and act as if I had practically no knowledge of the German language.

6

Chancellor Merkel receives a free tutorial on Germany's key role in the partition of an exotic continent

After breakfast, we took a taxi and headed for the Federal Chancellery, the seat of government and official residence of the German chancellor.

After about 20 minutes' ride through the busy streets of Berlin, we reached our destination.

The Chancellery is housed in a nine-storey main building that boasts two administrative wings. The imposing building boasts several columns of glass façades. From the information we gleaned from a leaflet containing information about the Chancellery, it is reputed to be the largest of its kind in the world, being eight times larger than Washington's White House.

After passing through security, we were asked to take our seats in a large reception area. After waiting for about a quarter of an hour, our attendant signalled us to follow her. After following her through a few doors and passageways, we were finally ushered into the office of the German chancellor.

Reputed to be the most powerful woman on Earth, she was simply dressed in a black-and-white pantsuit and wore a pair of simple black ladies' low-heeled leather shoes

On seeing us, she rose from her seat, walked towards us and vigorously shook the hand of each one of us and bade us take our seats.

After she had also taken her seat on a sofa facing us, she began to address us in a friendly manner through an English interpreter.

"Welcome to Berlin, I hope you are enjoying your stay in the German capital."

"Yes indeed, it is a lovely place!" we replied as if with a single voice.

"I am delighted to hear that. Now let us get to business", she said looking at us in turn. "To be honest with you, initially I was reluctant to meet you. I really thought you could present your petition to our ambassador in Accra and spare yourself the trouble of travelling all the way to Berlin. I reluctantly changed my mind when word reached me from our embassy in Accra that you have the official backing of your president.

"Now, dear gentlemen and respected lady, you are face-to-face with the German head of government. Please let me know what it is that led you to me?"

"Thank you very much, Madam, for granting us an audience", Douglas began. "It is indeed our African custom to allow the elderly to speak on such occasions. The leader of our delegation sadly did not get the opportunity of going to school. He has therefore delegated me to speak on his behalf.

"Before I move on", Douglas added, "please permit me to quickly introduce members of the delegation."

After a quick introduction of each of us, Douglas went on:

"Dear Madam, the traditional leader of our little village of Mpintimpi, in consultation with the Village Committee, has sent us to you to discuss some matters of importance relating to our community.

"We are ordinary peasants. The average daily income of all four of us put together barely adds up to one Euro. We have to struggle from the rising of the sun to its setting to make ends meet.

"Over the last several years we have hoped for an improvement in our living conditions – to no avail.

"We therefore decided to bring our pathetic plight to the attention of our president. Our main demand on him is to initiate steps towards the introduction of a welfare state system, similar to that which you have in your country. Our president, whilst not against the idea, pointed to the empty state coffers.

"Whilst citing internal factors to account for the desolate state of our finances, he also pointed to external factors.

"Among others, he called our attention to the tariffs as well as restrictive trading practices in place in the EU as contributing factors to our problems.

"He cited as an example the current trade arrangement involving Ghana's main export crop, cocoa. Whereas the country could benefit most if the raw cocoa were to be processed in the country itself and turned into the finished products such as chocolates, cocoa buttercreams, bread spread and other products before exporting into Germany and elsewhere, for some reason our trading partners prefer buying the raw beans than the finished products.

"He went on to cite the high interest we pay on loans granted our country by the developed world.

"Several such adverse external factors, he surmised, had led to our precarious economic situation. He made us understand that, despite several attempts on his part and that of previous governments, their pleas – our pleas – have fallen on deaf ears.

"After discussing the matter at a meeting of our Village Committee, it was decided that we take the matter into our own hands and travel to meet some of our trading partners to discuss the matter.

"You might very well ask us, why didn't you ask the Ghana representative in Berlin to petition us on your behalf?

"We did consider the matter. We decided against that option for the reason that should a representative of our government in your country turn up at your office well fed and clothed, you may not recognise the dire situation that ordinary citizens like ourselves find ourselves in.

"Now, you yourself are witness to how lean and underweight we are – this despite that fact that we have managed to pick up some weight since our arrival in your country a few days ago.

"As you can bear witness from his sad looks and bony appearance, our uncle, who has passed the age of 80 years, is not feeling exceptionally good. He has asked me to plead with you to do whatever is in your power to ensure he enjoys the barest minimum of a decent lifestyle during his remaining days on Earth.

"He also wants to spare his offspring the ordeal he has already gone through – the harsh living conditions that have been and continue to be the lot of residents of the village. That, in a nutshell, Madam, is the reason for our coming."

Mrs Merkel listened attentively throughout the time Douglas spoke. Though her secretary took notes, she, from time to time, did so too.

We waited tensely for her response. It came at last:

"Well, much as I sympathise with your cause, I am afraid there is little we can do for you. In the first place, I don't share your view that we are responsible for the economic difficulties of your country.

"We could eventually decide to help you out by devising a developmental package for your community. We usually prefer to deal on a government-to-government basis.

"If we decided to abandon that protocol and deal directly with you, it will set a dangerous precedent. In due time every single community in your country will be knocking on our door, asking for help. I would suggest you contact a charitable organisation – the German Red Cross, for example, instead."

"I want to point out to Madam that we are not requesting direct assistance", Douglas replied. "Instead, we are calling for the creation of favourable trading conditions for our country. That, it is our hope, will lead to an improvement in our economy, which in its turn will enable our government to introduce a welfare state system.

"Concerning the matter of who or what has contributed to the present state of affairs in our country, we do indeed agree with our president that Germany is partly responsible for our plight."

"In what respect is Germany partly responsible for the economic malaise of your country?"

"Even if Germany does not carry direct responsibility, she cannot exonerate herself from blame by virtue of her historic role in the affairs of our continent."

"I don't understand what you are driving at", she replied. "Historically, we held few colonies in Africa. We were forced to relinquish them to France and the UK following our defeat in World War I. You are from Ghana. I did some research ahead of your visit. It was called the Gold Coast until it gained its independence from Great Britain in March 1957. So actually, it is Britain you have to contact, not Germany!"

"Well, Madam, in our opinion you cannot entirely exonerate Germany of blame as regards our present predicament. Madam, you are certainly aware of the Berlin Conference of 1884–1885, aren't you?"

"Yes, of course; but what has that to do with our present discussion?"

"Before I answer that question, I want Madam to imagine the following scenario.

"The residents of Mpintimpi decide one day to invite the other surrounding villages in and around our settlement to a conference. During the deliberations, we pass a resolution to partition Europe among ourselves: Mpintimpi, which conceived the idea, assigns Germany to itself.

"Adadekrom, our next neighbour to the north, takes control over Holland: Afosu to the south takes over England; Amenamu to the south-west of us, takes control over Spain.

"Without your knowledge, the chiefs and elders of Mpintimpi come over to Berlin to put their plans into action.

"Though the initial plan involved taking complete control over the running of the country, because they find you a sympathetic and a friendly person, they decide to allow you to rule on their behalf. You have to account to them though. How would Madam react to such a scenario?"

"Hey, you poor peasants from a little African village dreaming of taking over a country! My strong army would blow you into pieces in no time!" She laughed good-humouredly.

"Well that is exactly what you did to Africa! Surely, you are aware of the Berlin Conference that led to the partition of Africa? Just to recap: 'To establish control over trade in Africa, Portugal called the conference and left it to Germany to arrange it, which she did with perfection, leading eventually to the holding of the conference in the Berlin residence of the Chancellor in 1884–1885.'

"This was done without consulting any resident of the continent, indeed without inviting any African to the table! The German emperor – well, he could even have been your blood relative – called a conference to partition Africa. In our view, the partition of Africa has indirectly led to the present predicament of our village, in particular, and Africa in general."

"I accept the historical fact you are alluding to. It is indeed true that my forefathers together with other world powers partitioned the continent among themselves without your direct involvement.

"About 60 years later, African countries, spearheaded by your country, Ghana, demanded and were granted independence by the colonial masters. In the case of Ghana, you have been independent for almost 60 years!"

She paused before continuing. "Now, before I continue", she said, "I want to digress just for a short while and take you back to another historical event. You appear to be a well-educated and eloquent individual, so I presume you are well informed on matters related to the World War II. My ancestors caused World War II. I am deeply sorry for the suffering that the rest of the world had to endure through the actions of Adolf Hitler.

"We inflicted suffering on the world; our actions brought suffering to us as well. I believe you are aware of the terrible destruction that followed; if not, I want to let you know that World War II left Germany in a complete rubble of ruined buildings. Almost every building you saw as you drove through the streets of Berlin was either reduced to rubble after the war, or did not exist at all at the end of the war in April 1945. But through sheer hard work we managed to rebuild our country within a matter of years."

"Madam, may I please interrupt you. You profited from the Marshall Plan, put in place by the victorious Allied Forces. Yes, the victorious allies of World War II, spearheaded by the US, pumped vast sums of money into your economy. You might not have managed to rebuild your country so quickly without the Marshall Plan."

"Look at this gentleman pointing to the Marshall plan as the sole factor leading to the rebuilding of Germany!" she smiled. "I do not dispute the fact that the Marshall Plan placed the money needed for rebuilding our country at our disposal. But think what would have happened if we had squandered the money and not put it to good use.

"I can point to a kind of Marshall plan in place in your country; what have you made out of it?"

"Which Marshall Plan?"

"Well, I could refer to it as a God-given Marshall Plan for Ghana and Africa at large. I have in mind the vast deposits of various precious minerals and other resources – petroleum, gold, diamonds, gas, uranium, you can go on mentioning them. Ghana, for example, used to be called the Gold Coast? Right or wrong?"

"Right."

"I guess the name stemmed from the fact that substantial amounts of gold were found there."

"You are right."

"The question worthy of asking then is – what has happened to the gold of the Gold Coast?

"Beside gold, your country is also blessed with diamonds, bauxite, magnesium, aluminium, etc. As if that were not enough, substantial amounts of oil have been discovered in your country. If in spite of all the listed natural resources, you are putting the blame for your present predicament at the doors of the Berlin Conference, then I am at loss as to how to react to that.

"If you like, I will place tickets at your disposal to offer you the opportunity to travel to the major cities of this country to witness for yourselves what we have achieved over the years. You may not believe it, but almost every major city here was razed to the ground – the result of war. It took us barely 20 years to rebuild.

"Ghana has been independent for 60 years – and yet now you are travelling the vast distance – crossing the Sahara, the Mediterranean, southern Europe to Germany – to blame us for your predicament?

"Concerning the partition of Africa that you referred to, I accept the fact that it was initiated in Berlin, but my question is – what is preventing you from coming together as a continent?

Indeed, what is preventing your leaders from joining forces together instead of each country going it alone?"

For reasons that he later refused to reveal to us, Douglas at that juncture decided suddenly to change the direction of the discourse.

"Madam, politics aside", he smiled, "I find you a very pleasant person to deal with."

"Ach, that was unexpected. Thanks for your compliment anyway."

At that stage, Mrs Merkel glanced at the clock on the wall.

"I am not trying to drive you out of my office. The fact remains though I have another meeting in about 10 minutes from now. We have five minutes to round off."

"We are grateful for the opportunity", Douglas said. "Before we leave, please allow us to express a final wish. We have been impressed by the excellent transportation network here in Berlin – the underground trains, the road network. Would Madam please consider sending some of your excellent road engineers down to our village to help fix a problem that has plagued the residents there for a considerable time? It involves the main road leading from our village to the next major town. Over the past 40 years, several attempts have been made to put the road in good shape – to no avail. We believe German engineering prowess will surely help fix the problem."

"I have taken note of the issue raised. I do really pity you, but I do not want to make any promises. We have an international development agency through which our foreign aid is channelled. Your country is a beneficiary of the scheme. I cannot interfere directly in the way funds are allocated. It is up to your government therefore to present their requirements. Should your government include the road you are referring to in their wish list it will be funded accordingly."

Just as we were about to depart, she turned to Adwoa and began: "Madam, I really love your colourful clothing!"

"Well, we tend to love colour in Africa", Adwoa smiled.

"I must confess – whenever I host African leaders, I am stunned by the colourful outfits of the ladies. I have been presented with a few such bright outfits by some of your leaders. Our bad weather rarely offers me the opportunity to wear them unfortunately!"

Thanking her for her time, we parted company with Mrs Merkel and headed for the exit. Moments later we were back on the street.

7

EU President Juncker and the free lecture on European colonial involvement in a southern neighbour

Our next stop was Brussels; our appointment with Mr Juncker, the head of the European Union Commission, was scheduled for 2pm the next day.

We were due to fly on a Ryanair flight from the Berlin Schoenfeld airport. The departure was a little after 8am the next morning. The plan was to spend the night in Brussels after meeting Mr Juncker and travel on a Eurocity train to London the next day.

Everything went according to plan. After a flight lasting about 90 minutes, we touched down safely at Brussels International Airport. We went through immigration without any difficulty.

It was a chilly and windy morning. We took a taxi and headed for the headquarters of the European Commission in the European quarter of the city.

After about 20 minutes' drive, the imposing Berlaymont building complex, serving as the headquarters of the European Commission, came into view. Located at Schuman roundabout at Wetstraat 200, Rue de la Loi, it was commissioned in 2015.

After undergoing security checks, we presented our invitation letter at the reception. Next, one of the reception staff asked us to follow him.

Thinking we were at home in French, he began addressing us in French. Noting from our facial expressions that we were at a loss to understand him, he switched to English: "You speak English?"

"Yes please", Douglas replied.

"Okay, we need to take the lift to the 13th floor – that is where the president's office is located."

Soon we were in the lift heading upwards.

On our arrival on the 13th floor, he turned to us and began:

"Please wait here; I will come for you shortly."

He returned in about 15 minutes.

"Please follow me", he urged us.

We did as requested.

Moments later we were ushered into the office of Mr Juncker. I will spare the reader a detailed description of how his office was set up. My impression was that it was not very different from that of the German chancellor.

He was seated behind his desk flipping through papers in a folder in front of him as we filed in.

Dressed in a navy-blue suit and a red tie, he welcomed us wholeheartedly into his office.

After the initial greetings, we made the reason for our visit known. We do not want to bore the reader with a repetition of the reason for our European tour. We just repeated almost exactly what we told the German chancellor, the only exception being that we sought to stress the collective responsibility of present-day Europe for historical injustices meted out to our continent by Europe.

Without going into details, we touched on the slave trade, European colonisation of the African continent, the adverse legacy of colonialism, etc.

From his facial expression he seemed uncomfortable with the lecture.

After dwelling on the historical injustices meted out to Africa by Europe, Douglas turned to the present.

"Sir, I want to turn the conversation to the issue of trade. In this connection allow me to draw your attention to the trade barrier put in place by your organisation, which makes it virtually impossible for our goods to compete in your market.

"Sir, apart from the tariffs imposed on the goods by the EU, the huge subsidies your organisation pay to your farmers makes it virtually impossible for us to compete with them.

"Next I would like to turn to the financial market. We hardly receive any investment from Europe. The same thing applies to developmental loans. In the rare instance that we are granted any, such loans attract high interest rates, not to mention the strings that are usually attached to them.

"Finally, Mr President, allow me to touch on an issue, which though not directly of your making, we find the need to bring to your attention. I refer to the millions, if not billions of Euros that corrupt African politicians, corporate bodies, business entities, steal from the African continent only to deposit them in various European banks.

"Mr President, whilst not assigning you or your organisation direct blame for the current state of affairs, in our view not much is being done by Europe and the Western world in general to stem the tide, indeed to prevent such appalling behaviour by the greedy, heartless individuals and organisations involved.

"We are hereby requesting, most urgently, that the EU takes steps to help repatriate such stolen monies back to their rightful owners – the poor, the maimed, the dejected, the handicapped, etc, on the streets of Africa. Your Excellency, whereas your countries and banks could do without such monies, the poor of Africa cannot."

If his facial expression was anything to go by, he appeared clearly embarrassed by the pointed accusations.

"Allow me to respond to some of the issues raised", he began. "To save time I will be very brief. Concerning the issues of tariffs, they do not target Africa in particular. They are there to protect our single market from unfair outside competition. You may not agree with me in the matter, but I find them completely in order.

"Allow me to draw an analogy. You tell me you are from a little village. Assuming you have borrowed money from the bank to go into crop farming in your village. After producing your crops, you realise to your dismay that outsiders have come to offer the same goods you produce at a far cheaper price than yours. The villagers line up to purchase the cheap products from the newcomers, leaving your products to go bad. How will you react to that?

"The EU has a single market mechanism in place among its member states that needs to be preserved – if need be, with the imposition of the tariffs you have referred to.

"On the issues of your country being offered loans at unfavourable terms, well the conditions are determined by the dictates of the international monetary system over which I have no control at all.

"On the allegation of individuals and organisations from Africa and elsewhere depositing their monies in our banks, it is not within my remit to dictate to the banks how they should go about their day-to-day business.

"You will also agree with me that, at the end of the day, the banks cannot force anyone to deposit money with them."

"But surely they have a moral responsibility to refuse to accept stolen money!" Douglas countered.

"With respect, gentleman, how do you expect them to know whether the money an individual is depositing with them is stolen?"

"Where there is a will, Mr President, there is always a way. Assuming I am the manager of a bank somewhere in the EU and a politician from a poor country in Africa turns up with suitcases packed with stacks of dollar notes! I will engage that individual in a conversation in order to establish the sources of the funds."

"And if the individual tells you they came by the money through the sale of their property, what will you do? Travel with that person to his country to establish the truth? My dear friend, in the real world, investigating such matters is not as straightforward as you might think.

"You also seem to create the impression that the EU is doing nothing to alleviate poverty and suffering in Africa. That is not the case. Indeed, just as we are speaking, various agencies of the EU are carrying out various developmental projects in various parts of Africa – including Ghana!"

"Mr President, we do not want to dispute that fact. But the fact remains that, as far as we are concerned, such aid packages are non-existent, for we have never benefitted from any.

"We do not want to claim to speak for every poor and deprived citizen of our country. We dare say with all certainty though that should your organisation send someone to any of the several slums of our country to ask the residents there if they have heard of any help from the EU meant for them, the response with all certainty will be an emphatic NO."

"Well, I am the president of the EU Commission, and I am aware we have a development aid budget for your country. You do not expect me to know exactly how each Euro cent designated for your country is spent by your government, do you?

89

"Back to the issue of money laundering from Africa and elsewhere into the EU. I want to assure you that the we are taking appropriate steps to address the matter."

At that juncture he turned to Adwoa. "Madam, how are you enjoying your stay in Europe?" She starred at him, not uttering a word.

Noticing the surprise on the face of their host on account of her apparent neglect of his question, Douglas came to her rescue.

"She doesn't speak good English. I will translate for her."

A broad smile registered on her face after Douglas translated Mr Juncker's question.

"Good, good, help, please Sir; me, my mother, brother, poor; poor!" she stumbled.

"We will do what we can to help", said Mr Juncker, assuredly.

Taking a glance at a large clock hanging on the wall facing him, he turned to us and began:

"Our time is up, I am afraid. Please convey my greetings to your president on your return, should you happen to meet him."

"We will pass your greetings on at the appropriate time. For your information, we are not heading directly back home. We are continuing on to the UK, to meet Prime Minster May."

"Really?"

"Yes, we want to discuss our concerns with her as well."

"Is it not enough that you have discussed them with the president of the EU Commission?"

"With no disrespect, Sir; we deem it necessary to discuss them with her as well. The British bear extra responsibility – by virtue of them being our ex-colonial masters."

"Hmm, I need to revise my knowledge of the European colonial involvement in Africa. To be honest with you I was not aware the Brits were your colonial masters."

"Indeed, they were."

"Um, I hope Mrs May favours you with the needed attention. She is currently so embroiled with matters relating to Brexit, I doubt whether she can concentrate on anything else."

"She has given her go-ahead for the meeting; I expect her to dedicate the required time and attention to our meeting as well."

Moments later, we bade farewell to Mr Juncker and made for the exit of his magnificent office. Soon we were back on the street of the city generally considered the de facto capital of the Euporean Union.

We spent the night at a budget hotel at the outskirts of city.

8

British PM Theresa May and the plain-spoken handicapped lady from afar

E arly the next morning we took the Eurostar and headed for London. That we were able to ride on a train from mainland Europe to the British Isles was something the other members of the team found difficult to comprehend.

I took my time to explain the fact that a tunnel had been built deep under the surface of the Earth to facilitate a rail link between continental Europe and the British Isles, for that purpose. As the train travelled through the tunnel, the facial expressions of my three compatriots could be compared to that of an individual scared to death by a sudden confrontation with a tiger.

It took a little over 35 minutes to cross over to the UK. The almost sixty-minute ride from Folkestone, a port town on the English Channel where we emerged from the Eurotunnel, to London was uneventful.

A relative of mine resident in London had offered to host us for a while, sparing us the need to travel to my home in Loughborough which is located about 170 kilometres to the north of London. He and his wife and their three school-going children aged between 6 and 12 years welcomed us with open arms into their four-bedroom home in Croydon in the southern outskirts of the British capital.

Everyone in the team expressed the desire to rest awhile following the stressful tour of continental Europe. Fortunately, our appointment with the British prime minster was three days away.

After resting the whole day following our arrival, I decided to take the team on a tour of the British capital. Top on the list of the attractions was Buckingham Palace. My team-mates were in particular fascinated with the practice of the "changing of the Guards" in the forecourts of her majesty's palace.

As we looked on with the crowd made up of visitors from all over the world, the newly arrived team of guardsmen, supported with music from a regimentalband, underwent a well-choreographed process of assuming responsibility for the guarding of the palace from the team about to end their duty session.

Though I had watched the ceremony on a few previous occasions, I was as exhilarated as the visitors from Mpintimpi watching the ceremony, which lasted for approximately 45 minutes, for the first time.

On a rainy day in the last week of April 2018, we left our home early in the morning and headed for our appointment with the British prime minister at Number 10 Downing Street, which, as we later learnt, has been the official residence of serving British PMs since 1735.

After undergoing security, a guard posted at the entrance opened the black door to the entrance and ushered us into the building.

The door opened into a hall with a chequered floor. We were led up a staircase to the first floor. Adorning the walls of the staircase were portraits of all the British prime ministers, apart from that of Theresa May herself.

"She will have her portrait displayed not long after she has left office – in keeping with the tradition that only past PMs are represented", our attendant told us, even before anyone of us asked him about the absence of the portrait of our guest.

Finally, we were ushered into her office, which is just a stone's throw from the living area. Seated behind a huge wooden table was the British PM. She was dressed in an elegant navy-blue skirt suit and wore a pair of black low-heeled shoes.

After exchanging greetings and engaging in small talk that centred on our experience with the unstable English weather, the conversation soon turned business-like.

"I understand you are from a little village in Ghana."

"That is correct", Douglas replied on our behalf.

"My secretary has given me the gist of what your visit is about. You are now face to face with Theresa May. You have the opportunity to present your case."

"Thank you, Mrs Prime Minster, for the audience", Douglas began. "We are happy that, despite your heavy schedule, you have found time for us.

"Madam, as you are aware, our country has had historical links with your country. I don't want to go into much detail. I want to give only a brief overview.

"Though British merchants and traders had been active on the Gold Coast as far back as the 15th century, the Gold Coast formally became a British colony in 1867. It remained so until it gained independence in 1957.

"After independence Ghana, the new name for the Gold Coast, chose to remain in the British Commonwealth. We have remained a committed member since then.

"I now turn to the main reasons for requesting this meeting. Over the last several years we, the poor residents of Mpintimpi, had hoped for an improvement in our lives – to no avail.

"We feel neglected by the whole world. Not very long ago the Village Committee met to deliberate the way forward. In the end, we sent a delegation to present our grievances to our president.

"Our cardinal demand on him and his government is for the introduction of a welfare state system as exists in your country and several other countries, to alleviate the suffering of the poor and vulnerable who have nowhere to turn to.

"I want, Mrs Prime Minister, to cite Uncle, the leader of our delegation as an example. He is over 80 years of age. There is no state pension or benefit system in place to take care of him. Madam, currently he has no income – nothing! He certainly would have starved to death, but for the willingness of extended family members – individuals who are themselves struggling to make ends meet – to share their food with him.

"Our president, whilst being sympathetic to the idea of a state-sponsored benefit system, pointed to the empty state of the country's coffers.

"He outlined several factors both internal and external that have led to the desolate nature of the state finances.

"Whilst accepting the dire need for efforts to be undertaken internally to remedy the situation, he stressed that such steps would barely make any impact without addressing the external constraining factors as well.

"Concerning the external factors, he pointed in particular to the unfair trade practices and adverse monetary policies and practices of the developed world vis-à-vis developing countries, including Ghana.

"He went on to state that, despite many representations made by Ghana and other developing countries to the developed world to change their unfair policies and practices towards poor countries, virtually nothing has changed.

"After reporting back to our elders in the village, it was agreed that we send a delegation to talk to our trading partners in the developed world about the matter.

"We have come not to beg for food, Madam. We are only asking you to use your influence in Europe in particular, and the developed world in general, to ensure our country is fairly treated, indeed to ensure we get good trade deals, good access to favourable credit, preferably interest-free credit.

"We are also told our country is heavily in debt. We are calling for the writing-off of these debts as well! Such a step will lead to an improvement in our economy, which in turn would lead to an improvement in our standard of living."

Douglas paused for a while to gauge her reaction.

"Have you finished your presentation?" she asked.

"Not really."

"I am afraid we do not have much time at our disposal. I suggest therefore that you hold on, whilst I respond to some of the issues raised. If, after the meeting, you feel not everything has been tackled, you are free to present a paper outlining the outstanding issues.

"For now, I would like to respond to some of the issues raised. Before I do that, however, allow me to make a short observation.

"You are right that the Gold Coast, now Ghana, used to be a British colony. That was over 60 years ago! We did not choose to end our relationship – it was rather your own free choice.

"'The black man is capable of ruling himself, of organising his own affairs' – so Kwame Nkrumah, your first president, told us bluntly to our faces.

"On another occasion, he also declared: 'We prefer self-government in danger to servitude in tranquillity.' Of course, I also share his sentiment. Indeed, I prefer the freedom to do whatever I choose to do rather than to be dictated to by someone else.

"My forefathers, unwilling to engage you in any bloody conflict, packed their bags and left you to take care of your precious land.

"As expected, you were delighted with the opportunity to rule yourselves. Just by way of getting myself acquainted with your country, I watched a short video clip of the independence celebrations in Accra. There were scenes of jubilations on the streets of Accra in the days leading to that momentous day. Foreign dignitaries travelled from all over the world to witness the independence celebrations of the first African country south of the Sahara. 'Ghana, we now have Freedom!' The special hi-life music composed for the occasion became a national hit. On the night of independence, the huge ecstatic crowd danced gracefully to the popular music, and they danced through the night.

"Don't you find it unfair on your part that 60 years on you come back to Number 10 Downing Street to point accusing fingers at the British PM for being responsible for the challenges facing you in your little village?"

"Madam, may I please interrupt you?" Douglas began. "While not putting the blame squarely at the doors of the UK government for our woes, I still hold to my assertion that your government cannot entirely exonerate itself from blame."

"How so?"

"Your government began placing several obstacles in the way of the newly independent Ghana right from day one of our independence!"

"Where is the evidence?"

"Was it a coincidence, Madam, that on the very next day after Ghana's independence, the price of cocoa, the main export crop of the country, fell dramatically on the world market?"

"My dear friends from little Mpi..Mpi..Mpi...please help me, I cannot get my tongue around the name of your village!"

"Mpintimpi!"

"Mpint..tii..tii.pi… Never mind, I'll pronounce it the way I can! Surely it is indeed unfair on your part to accuse my government of deliberately manipulating the international commodity market to your disadvantage. Surely you are not ignorant of the complex mechanism at work on the commodity market to influence and/or determine the price set for a product such as cocoa. If you were not, you wouldn't accuse my government of calculated manipulation in regard to the international price set for cocoa."

"I am not convinced about your explanation. The sudden fall in the world cocoa price just at the time of our independence, could not be solely due to the working of market forces!"

"What else could have caused it?"

"Though we do not have concrete evidence, we suspect foul play in the matter!"

"By whom?"

"Those wishing the failure of the newly independent African country! As we just stated, we have no evidence pointing to any individual or state. I am convinced though that the sudden price drop came too close on the heels of our independence for it to have been the work of sheer chance!"

"I find it unfair on your part to blame outside forces for your malaise. I would have thought you would first talk to your corrupt politicians!"

"I was just about to raise that issue, Madam. Of course, I am not exonerating our politicians from blame. Poor governance, incompetence, unaccountability, corruption, etc., on their part have contributed to the present dismal situation." At this juncture Douglas took the glass of water served him earlier on, drank a sip, placed it back on the table and continued his presentation. "Madam, a few days prior to our arrival in UK, the bi-annual summit of the leaders of the Commonwealth was held in London. Leaders of the Commonwealth, many of whom came

from Africa and other developing countries, were received with
pomp and pageantry. They were well fed, they slept in posh hotels, enjoyed a lifestyle millions of their compatriots back home
could only dream of!

"We are appealing to you, Madam, that you raise the issue of
good governance, accountability, transparency, etc., with them
during such meetings."

"Well, you must understand we need to abide by the rules of
diplomatic etiquette that bars us from poking our noses into the
affairs of other nations."

"Much as we agree with you on that matter, we still expect
you to find a way of turning up the pressure on them in an effort
to help bring an end to their nefarious activities.

"Yet another issue: it is no secret, Madam, that various
African leaders have stolen substantial sums of money from their
various state coffers and deposited them in banks in London and
elsewhere in Europe. Some of the stolen money has also been
invested in properties in London and elsewhere.

"We accept you are not directly in charge of the banks; nevertheless, you could have wielded your influence and prevented
that from happening."

"You are expecting far too much from the British prime minister. How do you expect her to know about everything that is
happening in the country! Indeed, how can I know what is going
on behind the curtains of each and every bank in this country?

"Not that we are keeping silent on the matter. Indeed, we
recently passed several pieces of legislation that have the goal of
curbing the practices you alluded to.

"It is not a one-way street though. It is up to your leaders to
play their part by introducing good governance, by putting effec-
tive checks and balances in place to check such malpractices.

"Recently I just chanced upon a headline in one of your
local newspapers that spoke of ministers in your country who

served in the previous administration receiving double salaries. Of course, I do not want to prejudge the outcome of the ongoing investigations into the matter. One can only hope that your justice system deals robustly with the allegations – carry out an impartial investigations and punish the culprits involved if a case is established against them.

"The rule of law must be seen to be working in your area. Assuming I decided to defraud this country in that manner, the next day, I would, without doubt, not only lose my job, but end up in jail.

"I am certainly not an angel. But the law works here. So, I dare not take advantage of my position to amass wealth. Unless of course I want to exchange the comfort of Downing Street for a prison!

"Concerning your own personal issues. Much as I do pity you, I am afraid there is little I can do to directly bring a change in your situation. I am elected by the British people to serve the interest of the British people. I am paid by the British taxpayer; obviously, I have to occupy myself, first and foremost with issues pertaining to the British people."

"I thought we shared a common humanity, so instead of saying 'British first', we would have preferred you to say instead: 'Humanity first!'" Douglas countered.

"Of course, I do recognise my humanitarian commitments. Indeed, Britain has been, and will continue to be, a champion of human rights. Let us assume something terrible happens in your country – a destructive earthquake; a terrible drought that leads to food shortages; an outburst of a terrible epidemic, like Ebola – leading to acute human suffering. In such situations, it is our good British tradition, indeed our humanitarian sense of duty, to offer urgently needed assistance.

"Though we are all human beings residing on a common planet, as you rightly alluded to, yet the reality on the ground is that we live in different countries; indeed, different sovereign states. In normal times international rules and norms demand that governments take responsibility for their citizens.

"I am aware you had your last elections in December 2016. If I happened to be in your country at that time, would you have permitted me to vote? Of course not!

"In the same way that Ghanaians would not permit Theresa May, a British national, to vote for your president, Theresa May on her part expects the president of Ghana to cater for the needs of Ghanaians. It is simple logic, isn't it?"

"Madam, we could spend the whole day debating such hot topics. Time obviously is not on our side. So please, allow me to move on to other outstanding issues.

"Our president mentioned the matter of trade barriers, tariffs on goods, high interests on loans, etc., put in place by rich countries to the detriment of poor ones. I want to delve into a little detail concerning the matter of loans.

"When we approach you for loans to purchase essential goods such as medicine to treat our sick, my understanding is that we are charged high interests on such loans. I find it difficult to swallow the matter, Madam. How, Madam, can anyone expect a country that is already struggling to make ends meet to pay interest, indeed high interests, on loans granted them by the affluent nations?"

"Well, gentleman, much as I understand your point, I am afraid, I am not the right person to raise such issues with. I suggest you take your case to the International Monterey Fund and the World Bank. As far as I know, they are the two main financial institutions that grant loans to developing countries such as Ghana.

"You may not believe it, but my country from time to time, also accesses the international financial market for credit. Such monies are not lent out interest free! No, we are also made to pay interest on them."

"Your government may indeed access the international financial market for short and long-term loans – but when you do so, your loans attract lower interest rates compared to that charged on loans granted to poor countries the likes of Ghana. The experts in the area refer to credit ratings. Wealthy countries like yours enjoy a favourable credit rating. On the other hand, a poor and deprived country like Ghana is assigned a poor credit rating. Thus, if the UK and Ghana apply for the same amount of money, your country could probably get your credit at a rate of 2%, whilst Ghana gets a rate of 7%.

"Just reflect upon that, Madam – the rich country that can easily bear the financial burden gets the loan for less, whilst the poor ones that can ill afford to bear the burden are asked to pay substantial interests on their borrowings!"

"I must admit I am quite astonished at your considerable knowledge on such matters. I took you to be ordinary peasants from a little African village. I expected you, for example, to be well versed in matters concerning cocoa cultivation. That you are quite well informed on the operation of the international financial market has frankly come as a surprise to me."

"Should I take it as a compliment?" Douglas smiled.

"However you wish!"

"Though resident in a village, I have kept myself abreast with the affairs of the world by way of my small transistor radio.

"Finally, Madam, as we mentioned earlier on, during our meeting with our president we raised the issue of Ghana adopting a form of the welfare state system. We want the UN to get involved by passing a resolution calling for a globally binding universal welfare state system. In this connection, we are appealing to the UK to use her influence in the Security Council to support our cause."

"A universal welfare state system, how do you expect that to function?"

"For example, the UN could set up a poverty alleviation fund to pay for the scheme."

"A poverty alleviation fund to pay for a universal welfare state system! My friends, you are calling for Utopia to descend from nowhere upon our imperfect world? You must be daydreaming!"

"I am speaking on behalf of the poor and downtrodden of Mpintimpi. People who are well fed may not have the need to think of revolutionary ideas to end hunger. Not so those who are directly affected, yes, those threatened with death through starvation!"

At this juncture one of the PM's assistants signalled that our time was up.

Just as we were getting ready to leave, contrary to the prior agreement to allow only Douglas to speak for the group unless a question was specifically directed to an individual, Adwoa raised her hand and gestured to be allowed to speak.

Was it because she was the only female member of the group, was it a result of her disability? Whatever the reason, Mrs May, despite having been prompted by her staff that our time was over, granted her request without hesitation.

"Go ahead, I am listening", she said, a broad smile on her face.

"Me, no good English, no good...English..." Adwoa struggled to find her words.

On hearing that, Mrs May turned to Douglas and began: "You speak the same mother tongue, don't you?"

"Yes, Madam", he nodded.

"Then let her tell you everything in your language and translate to me. I am really keen to know what exactly is on the mind of the only female member of your group. Please translate precisely what you hear; do not leave out anything, okay?"

Adwoa struggled to get on her feet to address the prime minister.

"You may be seated, Madam; you don't need to stand to address me."

Back in her seat, she began:

"Thank you very much, Madam, for granting us the audience.

"Yesterday we went on a sightseeing tour of London. In the process, we went window shopping in Harrods and other shops. I was really impressed at the sight of the abundance of goods of all kinds on display in the shops.

"I was even more dumbfounded at the sight of the large variety of canned foods of various types and kinds manufactured for your domesticated animals. Please, do not take me for someone who is an animal hater. On the contrary, I have a kind heart for them. Indeed, we also keep a few dogs, cats and other animals in our village.

"Still, the abundance of pet foods of various kinds and types led me to think – I may be wrong – that domesticated animals in your part of the world enjoy a higher standard of living than their human counterparts in our part of the world!

"Yet another issue that struck me. As we were driving around London yesterday, other members of the team translated to me a radio discussion going on at the time. It centred around healthcare for pets. From the discussions, it came to my attention that pets like dogs and cats are profiting from the advance of medical technologies available to residents of your country: these include CT scans, MRI scans, even advanced surgery such as hip replacement surgery.

"The disability in my left leg, Madam, came about from an injection in my large sciatic nerve by a quack doctor. Lack of money to take me to hospital led my parents to seek the assistance of such an individual. He administered an injection that led to the paralysis of the affected leg. Recently, I was asked to go for an MRI scan. I could not afford it!

"I want to reiterate; we are not animal haters. The fact still remains though that animals living in this part of the world enjoy better living standards, including better health care, as compared to human beings living in my little village and other poor areas of my country.

"Madam, I am not pointing the finger of blame to any individual. Instead, I am blaming Mankind, humanity as a whole. In my opinion, the fact that humanity has permitted the prevalence of a such a state of affairs should be a blight on the conscience of all of us."

There's no art to find the mind's construction in the face, to quote King Duncan in *Macbeth*, one of William Shakespeare's best-known plays. Yet, if the facial expression on Mrs May's face was anything to go by, she appeared to be deeply moved by what she had just heard. Picking a tissue paper from a drawer, she wiped a few drops that had gathered in her eyes.

"I have taken your concerns to heart", she began in a subdued voice. "Perhaps you are not aware – my father was an Anglican priest. I am not implying that I am a perfect Christian, but I do my best. It is indeed a world of contradiction. I can really feel what someone like you are going through. I will ask our representative to raise the issue of a universal welfare state scheme at the next opportunity at the UN Security Council. Mind you, we have only a voice. Major countries like the US would have to come on board if it were to have any chance of success."

We bade farewell to the British PM and headed for the exit. The moment we stepped out of the door of the world-renowned 10 Downing Street, I turned to Adwoa and began:

"Hey, you touched on a very sensitive issue! The English are known for their fondness of their pets. I don't know how they will react to your comments should they get wind of it."

"*Kan na wu*! [Say it as it is even if it means your death!]", she said, smiling. "Doc, that reminds me of Amma Owusuah, your late mother, who gained the nickname '*Kan na wu*!' for her outspokenness."

"She without doubt would have been proud of you had she been with us today", I smiled.

"Congratulations for hitting the nail on the head!" Kwootwe joined in the conversation, tapping Adwoa on the shoulder.

"I don't know how many visitors have succeeded in bringing the British PM to the point of tears!" Douglas said. "Our meeting without doubt will occupy her mind for a long time to come!"

On getting home, we reviewed the progress of our mission so far. Though we had not received any concrete offer of help from the three leaders we had met so far, it was too early to consider the mission a failure.

There was still one world leader to meet, President Trump. Though we would have preferred a meeting shortly after that with the British PM, the earliest slot available, we were told, was two weeks thereafter. Initially we had thought of turning the offer down and limiting our campaign to Europe. On further consideration we decided to accept the offer.

9

Going viral in a global village

We had made it our custom to purchase one of the national dailies to keep ourselves abreast of world events. I left home early the next day after our meeting with the prime minister and headed for a newsagent at the end of our street to carry out the daily routine.

As I took a look at the several newspapers on display to decide which to purchase, my attention was drawn to the headline boldly printed on the front page of one of them:

"ANIMALS HAVE A BETTER DEAL THAN HUMANS!"

I decided to take a closer look.

A four-member delegation from a small village in Ghana was received by the PM in Downing Street yesterday. They had been sent by their village committee to meet Western leaders to highlight their plight.

During their meeting with Mrs May, which lasted about half an hour, they drew the PM's attention to the daily hardships they and the other residents of the little settlement had to endure. They also pointed to the fact that, in their opinion, domesticated animals – cats, dogs, horses, etc., living in the affluent countries of the world – have access to better meals and healthcare than themselves and other slum dwellers in other parts of the globe.

While not blaming the UK, their former colonial masters, entirely for their predicament, they appealed to the PM to use her influence in the world, in particular her status as a permanent member of the UN Security Council, to bring about a change in what, in their view, constituted a blight on the conscience of humanity.

Without hesitation, I purchased the newspaper.

The report, as we later found out, was also carried by the online editions of the left-wing national dailies, and picked up by news outlets worldwide. Soon well-established networks and media outlets, the likes of the BBC, CNN, Fox News, etc., as well as less well- known local and regional networks, picked up the report and began to spread the message.

It was not spread only by conventional media. In a matter of time, it also became a social media hit, shared many times on platforms such as Facebook, WhatsApp, Twitter, etc.

Not in the wildest of our dreams could we have anticipated the huge media interest. As the message began to spread around the globe, requests for interviews poured in from all four corners of the world. From leading global news networks to less well-known regional and local newspapers, the requests for interviews came thick and fast.

We considered the whole affair a bit overblown, if not pure hype. What, after all, had we done beyond the ordinary?

Concerning our demand for the introduction of a welfare state – what else had we done other than to quote from the provisions of the UN Human Rights Convention?

As regards our raising the issue that domesticated animals in affluent societies were getting a better deal than human slum dwellers – was it not an obvious fact?

Nevertheless, we were not unhappy with the publicity. So long as it was serving our purpose, all well and good!

On every imaginable social media platform – Facebook, Twitter, Instagram, etc., groups were set up spontaneously to support the movement, indeed to demand the rights for the poor and downtrodden. Expressions of support came in from all the slums of the world. The hashtags #petsgettingbetterdealsthanhumans, #globalwelfarestateinitiative became two of the top trending twitter hashtags

In the meantime, messages of support and solidarity flooded into the e-mail inbox of the account associated with the website we had set up in response to the unexpected global popularity.

E-mail support messages reached us also from slum settlements all over the world – from Dhaka in Bangladesh, Sao Paulo in Brazil, Cairo in Egypt, Nairobi in Kenya, Mexico City in Mexico, Mumbai in India – to mention only a few.

For the sake of space, only a few of the numerous messages that reached us are reproduced here.

> *Dear Friends from little Mpintimpi.*
> *We send you greetings from Lagos, Nigeria. From the millions of the downtrodden of Africa's most populous country.*
>
> *Despite the huge resources of our country the majority live in abject poverty. Our leaders have a smoke-screen of sovereignty to keep us perpetually poor.*
>
> *Eh, my friends, some people are indeed greedy, eh! I tell you, one of our governors, in his greed, decided to keep the Bank of the USA in his home. Indeed, when the law-enforcement agents went to his home, they were shocked to the bone to discover the piles and piles of freshly printed dollar notes stacked up in one of the rooms!! At the same time that the dollars were being piled up there, others, including little babies, were dying for lack of money to purchase lifesaving medication.*

In my personal opinion, it is high time the UN took a second look at the concept of sovereignty of states. When it comes to a clearly establishment case of blatant neglect of the population by the ruling elite by way of naked plundering of state coffers or unrestrained looting of state property to the detriment of the impoverished general population, a mechanism should be put in place to enable the UN, even if temporarily, to restrict the sovereignty of states to enable the prosecution of the perpetrators by a neutral international body.

I do not know exactly how that can happen, but I trust the best brains of the world community to come up with practical and feasible ideas.

Notwithstanding how the UN goes about the issue of non-interference in the internal affairs of other nations, we staunchly back you in your fight to get the UN to legislate a minimum welfare package for every individual of our troubled planet.

Yes, you can count on our solidarity and support; your fight is our fight.

Indeed, it is our opinion that with concerted effort every soul on planet Earth could be guaranteed the very basics needed for a decent livelihood.

We want to join in the movement. We understand you have plans to organise a march on New York. We are with you all the way. Please keep us updated; we shall endeavour to send delegates.

Best wishes
Oluwa Babatunde,
Ajengule, Lagos, Nigeria.

From New York, came the following:

Dear friends of Mpintimpi,

We, the League of the Homeless of New York City, wish to congratulate you for bringing the plight of the poor of the world into the global limelight

Whereas we do accept that your situation indeed is deplorable, we want you also to be aware that there indeed is also poverty here in the US. Yes indeed, a considerable number of residents here struggle to make ends meet.

In your little village of Mpintimpi where you are all living in abject poverty, you can console yourselves with the thought that everyone or at least the overwhelming majority of people worldwide are in the same boiling pot of poverty.

Not so in our situation. For example, in our case, at the same time when we are spending biting cold winter nights under bridges, our gaze into the not far distant part of our city can behold the glitter and sparkle of extreme wealth on display!

In an environment where the majority are riding on bikes, we have been forced by circumstances beyond our control to crawl on all fours, my dear ones!

It is great that you are organizing a Global Poverty March to New York. We shall surely dispatch a large contingent to join you. Together we shall take over, if only for a few days, the UNO and let the world know how we can with concerted effort show poverty the door, not only temporarily, but for ever.
Ronald Carter,
Homeless Resident
New York City.

From the capital of Burkina Faso, Ghana's immediate northern neighbour, came the following:

Dear Friends,

A friend of mine has informed me of your campaign to highlight the plight of the poor and downtrodden.

Before I proceed any further, I want to say something about my own circumstances and background.

I was born healthy, but contracted polio at a young age, which led to me become paralysed in both legs. My lovely parents took care of me. Sadly, both of them died before I attained the age of 15 years.

Though my relatives did their best to cater for me, due to the fact that they themselves were struggling to make ends meet I resorted to begging on the streets to earn my living.

As you might expect, life on the streets is really harsh. I normally position myself at strategic locations at the major intersections in the scorching heat of the hot tropical climate. When the traffic comes to a halt due to a red light or congestion, I venture onto the streets, hopping alongside and in between the vehicles as quickly as I can, begging.

It is my hope that your campaign leads the world to take notice of us and take the necessary steps to mitigate our suffering. Together with other street beggars we are setting up a local branch of the movement. Please keep us updated on latest developments.

Yours in solidarity

Adama Sawadogo, Ouagadougou, Burkina Faso.

***

Not only did huge numbers of people and groups contact us to express their support and solidarity, a great deal of those who contacted us requested permission to join in our movement – even though we had up till then not considered setting one up.

As requests to join in the movement continued to reach us from all over the globe, and bearing in mind that we could not make any decision without the consent of our traditional leader, we thought it wise first to consult the chief and the Village Committee to seek their opinion in the matter.

Without further ado, I dialled Nana's mobile. On hearing what we had to say, he asked us to give him a day or two to confer with the Village Committee on the matter.

Two days later, as we were relaxing at home, Douglas's mobile phone began to sound. It turned out be the *Okyeame* of the village.

"The Village Committee has given you the go-ahead to act on behalf of the village in the way you find appropriate. We are all proud of you. Thank you very much for helping put Mpintimpi on the world map!"

Having received the blessing of the Village Committee to expand the movement globally, we deliberated on a suitable name for the movement. In the end we settled on Poverty Crusaders.

***

We urged our supporters in other parts of the world to form local groups with the goal of putting pressure on their respective governments, to support our call for the introduction of the barest minimum income support for every citizen of the planet.

To ensure the movement was sustained beyond the initial tide of enthusiasm, we decided to organise annual meetings to discuss cross-border initiatives towards the attainment of our goals and objectives.

For the current year, we resolved to hold a global march on the UN headquarters in New York to culminate in what we christened "the UN General Assembly of the poor and downtrodden".

We decided to write, without delay, to the UN secretary general to inform him about our plans and to entreat him to place the UN facility in New York at our disposal.

To put pressure on him to decide favourably regarding our request, we decided to make the letter public. Towards this goal we published our plans on our social media platforms and urged our supporters around the globe to share it with their respective/ various groups.

Without further ado, we set our plans into action.

Was it a result of the worldwide publicity we had gained? Was it a recognition of the fact that the poor needed at last to be heard? Whatever the reason behind the UN secretary general's decision, the fact remains that barely a week after we had despatched our e-mail, we received an e-mail from the UN to the effect that our request had been granted.

The world body agreed not only to put the UN premises without any costs at our disposal; it also agreed to bear the costs of the boarding and lodging of participates during the three-day meeting! With the world body having offered to bear the costs of our boarding and lodging, what remained was the expenses involved in bringing delegates from all over the world to New York.

Soon, we began a campaign to get sponsors to help with the transportation costs.

Carried on a wave of unprecedented global goodwill towards our cause, offers of financial and material support began to pour in – from governments, philanthropic organisations, charities, and celebrities the world over. We also received help in kind – a number of airlines, including some of the most well-known names, offered to convey passengers free of charge to the meeting.

10

A crash course in royal protocol ahead of a once-in-a-lifetime excursion to Buckingham Palace

A few days after our meeting with Mrs May, we had just finished enjoying our breakfast and were planning a sightseeing trip when my phone began to ring. Since the number on display was not familiar to me, I wondered who was on the phone.

The caller identified herself as a clerk at the PM's office. She had a letter for us. Since it was an urgent matter, she wanted to know whether we were still in London, in which case she advised us to pick it up from the office as soon as we could.

What could it be, we wondered after the call ended? Douglas and I decided to quickly go and pick it up, whilst Kwootwe and Adwoa stayed behind. After changing underground trains a couple of times, we finally reached the office.

After exchanging greetings with the official, she turned to us and began:

"Yesterday the PM held her usual weekly meeting with the Queen. During their discussions, the PM informed Her Majesty about her meeting with you. To the utter surprise of the PM, Her Majesty expressed a keen desire to meet you! The PM has subsequently authorised me to arrange a meeting between you and Her Majesty the Queen. I do not know your plans, but I have been informed Her Majesty will be in London the whole of next week. As you may expect, she has a very busy schedule. Since she is keen on meeting you, her staff will find a way of squeezing your visit into her schedule."

"A meeting with the Queen! Hello! Did I hear you properly, Madam?"

"You heard me right, Sir. Her Majesty the Queen has granted your team an audience. We only need to agree on the time."

"We are at Her Majesty's service, day and night, at any time!" we stated as if with one voice.

"Two very dutiful subjects of Her Majesty's indeed!"

Eventually the appointment was scheduled for the following week, giving us a few days to prepare for the meeting with the head of the Commonwealth.

On breaking the unexpected news to the rest of the team, Adwoa was the first to react.

"The Queen? Who is the Queen?" she inquired.

"Wow! Never heard of Queen Elizabeth of England, Adwoa?" said Douglas.

"You expect someone who grew up at Mpintimpi to be familiar with things happening in faraway England, eh?"

"I did not say you have to know her. I am only surprised you have never heard about her!"

"Well Adwoa, I also grew up in Mpintimpi, yet I know the English Queen – in person, I must say!" Kwootwe joined in the conversation.

"You know the Queen in person? How and when did you meet her?" Douglas inquired.

"During her visit to Ghana in 1961. At that time, I was doing an apprenticeship in Kumasi. A huge *durbar* was held in her honour at the sports stadium. It was on that occasion that I saw her at close range."

***

The prospect of having an audience with the Queen in Buckingham Palace was daunting, to put it mildly. Personally, since moving to the UK, I had fancied the prospect of meeting the Queen in person one day. Never in the wildest of my dreams did I ever imagine it could ever happen.

After the reality of our meeting with the head of the Commonwealth had sunk in, we battled with the thought of how to prepare for it. How could we come by attire suitable for the occasion? It is superfluous to mention here that none of us had any.

We could in theory go shopping for some. Apart from the drain on our meagre resources, we did not want to appear before the monarch dressed as Europeans. Instead we wanted to dress in typical Ghanaian fashion, to highlight our traditional clothing.

As we deliberated on the matter, I came up with the idea of contacting the Ghana High Commission in London on the matter. Without delay I picked up the phone and requested a meeting.

The lady we were introduced to, Florence, could hardly believe what she heard from us.

"That is an honour not only to yourselves and your little village. We shall do our best to help you. I am happy to lend my own personal attire of Kente cloth to Madam. Looking at her size, I am sure it will fit her. Concerning the three gentlemen, I think we have a piece of clothing that the ambassador uses for ceremonial occasions. We still need two. Wait a minute whilst I make a few calls."

As we waited, she began making calls. After spending almost half an hour on the phone, she finally found a pastor of a Ghanaian church who promised to lend us the two pieces of Kente clothing requested. The plan was to call at the consulate two days later to collect the clothing items.

We called on the consulate two days later to pick up the items. As we were about to leave, Florence turned to me and began:

"Are you familiar with the royal protocol?"

"What royal protocol?" we inquired as if with a single voice.

"Visitors to the Queen are expected to comport themselves and behave in accordance with the traditions and rules of etiquettes of Buckingham Palace."

"No, we the common folks of little Mpintimpi have no ideas of such matters", said Douglas, laughing.

"We will arrange for someone to coach you. Though you will be visiting as private individuals, it is in our interest to ensure no mishap takes place, however minor, during your interactions with the monarch. The English press, especially the tabloids, is known for being raucous and inclined to sensationalism. Any mishap caused by you could be picked upon by them and blown out of proportions. It could cast a shadow not only on your growing international reputation, fame and status, but also on the honour of our country as a whole. Favourable press coverage of your visit, on the other hand, will cast a good light not only on your campaign, but also benefit the country as a whole."

As promised, two days prior to our meeting, we met a representative of the High Commission to familiarise ourselves with royal protocol. In a nutshell, the following was what we were taught:

We should make it a point to arrive at the palace several minutes ahead of time. Our meeting was scheduled for 11:30am. We were advised to err on the side of caution and arrive an hour ahead of time.

We were to address the Queen as "Your Majesty" at all times.

Adwoa, being female, would have to curtsey, that is to bend both knees with one foot in front of the other. In view of her disability, it would be sufficient for her only to bow her head before Her Majesty.

We were strictly urged to refrain from the following:

- to offer our hands in handshake unless she offered hers;
- to touch Her Majesty;
- to start the conversation (not to talk unless spoken to);
- to take our seats ahead of her;
- to form a straight line when standing in front of her. (We were told instead to form a semi-circle facing her, to facilitate the conversation.);
- to turn one's back to the Queen – it is considered rude;
- to take pictures when you are visiting her at home;
- to ask personal questions;
- to get carried away.

We were also told to meet her empty-handed. We had planned on taking some African craft as a present. This had to be handed over to the palace attendants rather than presented to her in person.

Though it was irrelevant to our visit, we were told that those invited to dine with her are not expected to start eating until she does.

And so we were ready for the all-important meeting with Her Majesty the Queen.

11

Her Majesty the Queen and the gold-studded earrings

We arrived at Buckingham Palace far ahead of our scheduled slot, which was 11.30am. We reported to the reception. After undergoing security checks, we were asked to follow a palace attendant, whose age I put at around 35. He led us along a long hall towards a closed door. The door opened into a large hall which, as we later found out, is known as the Queen's Audience Room. Standing in the middle of the room, a small bag hung from her wrist, was Her Majesty the Queen of England, Head of the Commonwealth.

She wore a light pink summery floral print dress featuring a delicate jasmine print in green and white. She matched this with a three-string pearl necklace and pearl earrings. Completing the outfit, the head of the Commonwealth chose a pair of black low-heeled court shoes.

The attendant bowed his head slightly and began:

"Your Majesty, I have the pleasure of introducing the distinguished guests from Mpintimpi, in Ghana."

As already practised, we quickly formed a semi-circle facing her. Adwoa, supported on her elbow crutch, approached her to bow her head as already practised. Whether it was out of nervousness or excitement, she actually bent forward rather than bowed! I had to struggle to keep my composure and resist the urge to burst out in laughter.

"Welcome to Buckingham Palace. I hope you are enjoying your stay in our country", Her Majesty said after she had gently shaken the hands of the other members of the group.

"Yes indeed", we replied in unison.

"And the weather?"

"To be honest, not really, Your Majesty", Douglas smiled.

"I can fully understand that. Our mostly chilly, foggy and rainy weather is nothing in comparison to the glorious weather in your country."

"Your Majesty, until my arrival here, I tended to complain about our persistently hot weather. After experiencing the UK weather, I will complain less about our weather in future."

"I love your country. I have been there on two occasions. I have really fond memories of my first visit. If my memory serves me right it was in 1961."

"If I may come in, Your Majesty, you arrived in Ghana on Thursday November 9, 1961", Kwootwe stated, smiling.

"My goodness! You remember the exact date!"

"Yes indeed. I was a teenager at that time; the whole country was in a state of ecstasy in expectation of your visit."

"That surely is no exaggeration on your part. I am used to crowds lining up on streets to greet me; the reception I received wherever I travelled in Ghana, especially on the day of my arrival in the country, was beyond the ordinary. Right from the airport, a long a distance of – I imagine – two miles to my accommodation in the city centre, a large and tumultuous crowd lined the route waving the Union flag as well as the Ghana flag."

"I am delighted to know Your Majesty enjoyed her stay."

"Oh, I did. I still have fond memories of the ball held in my honour on the first Saturday at the State House in Accra. We were entertained to live hi-life music. I danced to a tune of hi-life music with President Nkrumah.

"From Accra, we flew by helicopter to a major town in the north – I don't remember the name any longer.

"Tamale; it is a major town 620 kilometres to the north of Accra", Douglas said.

"Tamale, indeed! I can now recall how my husband and I were introduced to a fascinating mix of traditional African drumming, music and dancing all the way from the airport to the *durbar* grounds. Our next stop from Tamale was Kumasi, the Ashanti capital."

"You cannot imagine it, Your Majesty! I saw you at close range on that occasion."

"Oh, you did?"

"Indeed. I was 15 years old at that time. My father had sent me to do an apprenticeship in driving, what we call 'a driver's mate'. On the day of your visit hardly anyone went to work. My boss, who like myself was keen to see you in person, stayed away from work. I and some of my peers got up early in the morning to travel to the *durbar* grounds at the Kumasi sports stadium. Our effort was rewarded, for we got seats at a strategic location just overlooking the VIP podium. Everyone, I included, was ecstatic as the motorcade of our distinguished royal guest made its way through the gate, with President Nkrumah in his black suit standing beside you.

"As you alighted from the vehicle and walked to the *durbar* grounds with President Nkrumah beside you, we were sitting only a few rows away!"

"Really?"

"Yes indeed. May I, Your Majesty, ask if you still remember what you wore on that occasion?"

"Oh, that is several years ago!"

"I still have you before my eyes."

"That is remarkable."

"You wore a yellow short-sleeved simple but attractive summer dress, and a lovely yellow bucket hat. Hanging on your left forearm, just beneath the elbow, was a magnificent white leather handbag. You wore white high-heeled shoes to match the colour of your bag. You wore a pair of white gloves that extended to just below the elbow. Then, as part of your attire for that memorable occasion, you wore brilliant gold-studded earrings as well as a pearl necklace comprised of three strands, creamy in colour and fastened with a small diamond clasp!"

"That's amazing! You have without doubt a photographic memory."

"Your Majesty, I am not trying to blow my trumpet before the whole world. Those who know me say exactly that about my memory. If I had had the opportunity of attending school, I could have made it far on the academic ladder."

"Why didn't you go to school?"

"My parents did not have the means to pay for my education. Even if they had the means, things would not have been easy. The nearest school was several miles away. They would have had to look for someone who was prepared to allow me to stay with them during the week."

"That is sad indeed."

"Your Majesty, things don't look good for us. I have, since my childhood not known anything apart from poverty and want. I am sure the PM briefed you concerning the reasons for our trip. It is our hope that Your Majesty, as head of the Commonwealth, will do what she can to support our cause."

"Certainly. My prime minister informed me about your case in our last weekly meeting. Your story, especially that of Madam, has touched all of us. We shall do what we can to help."

At this stage the palace attendant, the same individual who had ushered us in, entered. Bowing his head slightly, he reminded the Queen concerning the arrival of her next guest.

"Oh, time has flown by very quickly; I didn't even have time to offer you seats. I must say I did enjoy your company. My PM has briefed me about the reason for your visit. She is a very kind-hearted individual. I trust she will do whatever is within her power to help you achieve your goal. It is indeed sad that, whereas many are enjoying the sunny side of life, others struggle… to make ends meet.

"I wish you all the best in your endeavours. I am sure you want to capture scenes of our meeting to show to your people."

"Your Majesty, that is our hearts' desire."

"It is not usual protocol to do that; on this occasion, however, I am happy to grant an exception. The residents of your village should know how proud you have made them."

At that moment, one of the attendants left the room, to appear a few minutes later with a camera in his hand.

Moments later a *click, click* sound could be heard as he took pictures of the meeting.

Thanking Her Majesty for her kindness, we parted company from the monarch.

As we stepped out of the audience room, we walked along the corridors and headed outside. The assistant who took the pictures approached us and handed Douglas a small envelope.

"Enclosed is a pen drive storing digital versions of the pictures taken with Her Majesty. They are amazing; I'm sure you will like them."

"Thank you very much!" we said as if with one voice.

Throughout the rest of the day, our conversation centred on our meeting with the Queen.

How could anyone of us have imagined at the onset of our mission that we would end up meeting the Queen?!

12

Out-of- the- ordinary royal wedding guests yearn for a tête-à-tête with their royal hosts

Was it a special treat from Her Majesty the Queen? Was it a result of the media attention; or was it a mixture of both? In any case, just as we had finished our breakfast one morning, we heard a knock on our door. It turned out to be the postman.

"I have a special delivery for you, requiring a signature", he stated

"Really?" I replied, taken aback, since I was not expecting anything special.

I wondered where it had come from. The royal seal on the envelope led me initially to think it was a follow-up from our visit to Buckingham Palace. Was the Palace writing to express the Queen's thanks for our gift?"

As I hesitated to open it, Adwoa snatched it from my hands and tore it open without delay.

Enclosed in it was a magnificent card with "Harry & Meghan" printed boldly on it!

"Harry and Megan? Who are they?" Adwoa inquired.

"Really? You have no idea who they are?" said I.

"This time I am also at a loss as to who they are", Douglas confessed.

"Well, Kwootwe will keep himself out of this! If Douglas, our 'Professor' has no idea, what do you expect an uneducated old man like me to know?"

Douglas snatched the card from Adwoa, unfolded it and began to read aloud:

> *"We take pleasure in inviting you to our Wedding on Saturday May 19, 2018 at 11am at the St George's Chapel, Windsor Castle."*

"An invitation to attend the Royal Wedding!" I exclaimed. "Woo hoo! That must be an April fool's joke!"

"Doc, today is not April 1; so why do you think it could be an April fool's joke?" Douglas asked.

"I don't understand what it is all about", Adwoa protested. "Can you please explain the matter, Doc? Who are Harry and Megan to begin with?"

"Well, pay attention as I explain. Harry is the grandson of Her Majesty the Queen. He is fifth in the line for the monarchy. He is engaged to Meghan. They are marrying on 19 May. Apart from their close relatives and friends, only highly distinguished personalities and celebrities are invited."

"Is the invitation meant for you alone, Doc?" Douglas enquired.

"No, it is meant for all four of us; indeed, our names are printed on it."

"How did they get to know of us?"

"Are you surprised? Whether we like it or not, by virtue of the recent popularity we have gained, our names have become part of the public domain. I read in the news that they were inviting 2,000 members of the public to the palace grounds. But to think that we should be part of the privileged is beyond belief!"

"That is indeed a real honour, not only for ourselves but for Mpintimpi as a whole!"

Just then Douglas, who had snatched the card from my hands to read it for himself, exclaimed at the top of his voice:

"Friends, this is just incredible! It is like a fairy tale come true!"

"What is it about?"

"You just take a closer look; you thought we had been invited to witness the event from outside the church, but that does not seem to be the case."

At that moment I snatched the card from him and read the content again.

Douglas was right! I had overlooked the line: "You are part of the 600 guests invited to witness the wedding from within the St George's Chapel. We look forward to seeing you."

"We are invited to the wedding of M&H in the historical St George's Chapel on 19 May 2018!" I shook my head in disbelief. "To be among the nearly 600 guests, including A-list celebrities and senior royals, is an opportunity none of us in the wildest of our dreams could have envisaged or imagined. How are we to prepare for such an historic occasion?"

If the invitation could only have come two days earlier, we could have begged the Ghana High Commission to permit us to use the same clothes for the wedding, and not have returned them the previous day.

Who else could we contact, apart from the Ghana High Commission? Moments after reading the card, Adwoa was dialling the number to the Ghana Embassy.

No one answered the phone; she was instead asked to leave a message. She did as requested. After waiting several hours in vain for a call back, we decided to call again. This time the phone was picked up – not by the same lady we had been dealing with before, but by her deputy. She informed us she was deputising for her colleague who was on sick leave.

Fortunately, the clothes were available, so we were asked to pick them up during working hours.

Leaving Adwoa and Kwootwe behind, Douglas and I left the next day to collect the clothes.

***

We left early and headed for Windsor Castle in Berkshire where the wedding was to take place, all of us adorned in beautiful, colourful Kente clothes.

It was a glorious day. As if heaven was giving its seal of approval to the event, the sun, which cannot always be counted upon to show up in skies above the British Isles, had decided to grace the occasion not just with its presence, but with its very special bright, benevolent side.

We had decided to err on the side of caution, so left for the occasion very early. In the end we arrived at the grounds two hours ahead of time.

A large crowd had already gathered along the streets of the little town at the time of our arrival.

From the internet, I had gleaned a short background history of Windsor Castle. Built nearly 1,000 years ago, it serves as the principal castle for Queen Elizabeth II. St George's Castle Chapel, where the ceremony was to take place, was established in the 14th century by King Edward III.

Words can hardly describe our joy and exhilaration, triggered by the opportunity to be part of the momentous event. There were no doubt millions in the UK and elsewhere on the globe who would have cherished the chance of witnessing "M&H" tying the knot on a gorgeous day at St George's Chapel in Windsor Castle. To be part of the nearly 600 guests, including

A-list celebrities and senior royals, was a once-in-a-lifetime experience none of us would ever forget.

Since we were well ahead of the time, we decided to take our position at one corner of the street to while away the time before going into the chapel.

As we were enjoying the scenery and conversing about various issues, a lady who stood not far from us turned to Adwoa and began:

"Excuse me for my curiosity, but are you related in any way to Meghan?"

"Huh! Can you please repeat the question?" Adwoa said, not believing her ears.

"I mean, are you related to Meghan, are you a cousin, perhaps?"

"Goodness! I wish I were!"

"No?"

"No, indeed. Do I look like her?"

"Yeah, I see a striking similarity."

At that juncture Douglas joined in the conversation.

"Madam", turning to the stranger, "you are really a good observer, I must say. It did not occur to me until you put the question. Now looking at my sister critically and comparing her face with that of Meghan's as displayed on the invitation card, I do indeed discern an astonishing similarity! The chin, the cheeks, the eyes, the forehead, the hair… Even the way she smiles – the similarities are conspicuous!"

"Who knows, both might share a common ancestry!"

"Well, that cannot be ruled out, can it!" I said. "That brings to mind the time when I was a student at Hanover. I attended a conference organised by students from the developing world. Many of those attending thought I and a participant from Jamaica, whom I was meeting for the first time, were brothers! Blood is thicker than water, as they say! He could of course be the offspring of an ancestor of mine sold into slavery from the then Gold Coast."

A look at the time told us it was time to proceed to the church. After presenting our invitation card, the usher led us to our seats. Seated comfortably in the pew of the church, which according to our information dated back to the 15th century, we looked forward eagerly to the start of the historical wedding ceremony.

About 15 minutes after our arrival, the bride and her mother arrived. Meghan Markle was accompanied by two pageboys who held up her train as she made her way up the chapel steps. She was wearing a simple, long-sleeved white dress with a veil covering her face.

As she entered the chapel, a fanfare was played. Her elaborate veil was embroidered with flowers. It had been embroidered at Meghan's request, as we later learnt, with flowers that came from each of the 53 Commonwealth nations.

Her soon-to-be father-in-law, Prince Charles, the Prince of Wales, accompanied her to the altar.

Moments later, Prince Harry, wearing his military uniform, joined his bride at the altar.

The officiating pastor, who we later learnt was called Bishop Curry, the first African-American presiding bishop and primate of the Episcopal Church, had travelled specially from the US to assume the role.

After preaching a memorable sermon that centred on the theme of 'the power of love', the much-awaited moment arrived.

As "H&M" gazed into each other's eyes and exchanged vows, the archbishop joined their right hands together and said: "Those whom God has joined together, let no-one put asunder." Loud cheers could be heard from outside St George's Chapel as the Archbishop of Canterbury proclaimed them husband and wife.

The service ended with the national anthem. The newlyweds kissed on the steps of St George's Chapel as onlookers cheered.

After the wedding, the newlyweds, cheered on by tens of thousands of their enthusiastic fans and well-wishers, were driven away in an open horse-drawn carriage in a procession through the streets of Windsor.

As part of the specially invited guests, we were invited to a reception.

How much we would have cherished the idea of getting, even for a few minutes, the chance to chat directly, even for a short moment, with the newlyweds and to thank them for the honour of permitting us the privilege of witnessing at first-hand the historic occasion – but unfortunately that was not possible.

As we drove home Adwoa suddenly turned to us and began:

"Why not extend an invitation to "M&H" to visit Mpintimpi one day?"

"Are you dreaming?"

"No. I am serious!"

"Do you have anywhere for them to sleep?"

"I am not expecting them to sleep in Mpintimpi. They could stay at a hotel at Nkawkaw."

"My good sister, apart from Accra and perhaps Kumasi, I don't think there are any other towns in the country boasting the type of hotels suited for the royal couple."

"We could arrange for them to stay in a luxury hotel in Accra. They could leave for the village early in the morning, spend a while talking with us and return to Accra in the evening."

"Well, as the saying goes, 'there's no harm in trying!'"

"How can I get the invitation to them?"

"I suggest you drop it at the British High Commission in Accra, to be passed on to them on our return."

"I will certainly give it a try."

13

A deal-maker president and the "deal of the century."

The flight from London Heathrow to Washington Dulles International Airport was uneventful, as were the immigration checks.

We travelled by taxi to our hotel, a budget hotel about half an hour's drive from the airport.

After dinner, we rehearsed for our meeting at the White House. That President Trump, despite his busy schedule, had agreed to meet us was in itself a cause for optimism.

What were we to expect? His usual frank talk? Was he going to say something controversial, something that would cause irritation not only at home but also abroad?

We agreed to stick to our usual plan and leave Douglas to speak on our behalf, unless the president put a question directly to any of us.

Early the next morning we took a taxi and headed for the White House. The taxi driver told us he had driven passengers to the location so many times he did not need to feed the address, 1600 Pennsylvania Avenue, into his GPS.

"I can drive you there with my eyes closed", he said, smiling. "I am a little over 50. I started driving a taxi in the Washington area when I was around 20. I think it was towards the end of the Reagan presidency. Then came Bush senior, to be followed by Clinton, then Bush junior, followed by Obama… now, hey, Trump! Eh, President Trump! My friends. I better keep quiet!"

Without revealing we were on our way to see him, Douglas inquired: "How do you find him?"

"I am not interested in politics; I only wish that someone would close his Twitter account!"

"But you cannot do that! It will amount to a breach of his human rights!"

"Okay, then they had better employ someone to play the role of a filter for him – just exactly what you do when you pour your dirty water on a paper filter to remove the dirty stuff, don't you? In the same way they should pay someone to filter out all the unwanted stuff from his tweets! I am a taxi driver, a common man on the street as it were. I can say something insulting, people may not like it, but they won't put so much weight on it. Not so the president. His words carry weight.

"Anyway, friends, let's talk of something else. The weather for example; it promises to be a sunny day today."

"I have been pleasantly surprised by the weather."

"Why so?"

"We are from Africa. We arrived here not long ago. We hear at home your weather is very bad, so that was what we were expecting. Since our arrival, however, we have had nothing but good weather!"

"Friends, you have come at the right time. You better not venture here in winter, between December and February. It can indeed be very cold here; not only that, there can be terrible snow."

"I wish I could experience snow!" Adwoa joined in.

"Well, then come here in winter; but be sure you come with very warm clothing, not the type you are wearing now."

After about half an hour's drive, our chatty driver dropped us at a spot several metres away from the gate of the White House.

After going through extensive security checks, we were asked to wait in a reception area.

After waiting for about 10 minutes, a lady wearing a chic red dress and high-heeled shoes, which produced an audible *click-clack* sound as she walked, entered the room.

"Visitors from Mpintiiimiipiii?"

"Yes please."

"Your IDs please."

We produced our identification papers as required.

"Please follow me", she said after cross-checking our passport details with a sheet of paper she held in her hands.

Accompanied by the lady who, according to information we later received, was a secret service agent, we were ushered into the Oval Office. Seated behind a huge wooden table adorned with the US flag was President Trump himself. I would have recognised him anywhere, even on the street without any introduction.

Unlike our meetings with European leaders, he remained in his seat until we approached his desk. He then got up, shook our hands and asked us to take our seats.

We had barely settled in our seats when he turned his attention to Adwoa and began:

"What happened to you, Ma'am?"

"Sir. I do not actually have a recollection because it happened at a tender age. My parents tell me I fell sick and they had no money to take me to hospital; then someone came to the village who attended to me, who gave me an injection; shortly thereafter I was unable to move the affected leg. That has been my lot ever since."

"That is terrible; very horrifying. Did you receive any compensation?"

"Nothing; sir – not even money to take me to hospital."

"That is bad, really bad. It is a really cruel world. Bad things happen to good people."

A short silence followed, broken by the president.

"Now folks, let's get to business. I have been briefed by my aides about your coming. I know it is about deprivation, hunger, poverty and similar stuff. I want however to hear the matter from the horse's own mouth. So, what has brought you all the way from Guyana to the White House. "

"Just a point of correction, Mr President. We are from Ghana and not Guyana."

"Oh boy, the Donald has again confused matters! I really thought I was receiving visitors from Guyana!"

"Mr President", Douglas began, "Guyana is in South America, located between Venezuela and Surinam. Their capital is Georgetown. We on the other hand are from Ghana in Africa. It used to be known as the Gold Coast. The name was changed to Ghana after it gained independence from the British in 1957."

"The Brits were at your place as well?"

"Yes sir."

"The Brits, they were everywhere! Well, in effect, I am also partially British. My mother was Scottish; she moved to the US almost a century ago. But it wasn't the Scots who went about colonising others. They went out as missionaries. It was rather the English who set up colonies."

If he expected any of us to react to that, he might have been disappointed, for none of us reacted to his remarks.

"Okay, folks, what can I do for you?" he resumed after the short break.

"Mr President, we live in a little village in Ghana. Life is very harsh there. We have waited over the years for our government to help us – to no avail. We have therefore taken upon ourselves a mission to bring our plight to the attention of influential leaders like yourself.

"We want you to use the influence of the US in the United Nations, to put the necessary mechanisms in place to ensure that we, the poor of Mpintimpi and elsewhere in the world, are provided with the basic daily needs required for human existence – a daily supply of food and water, decent accommodation, basic health care, basic education, etc."

"Wait a minute", the president interjected. "Before I respond to your call for a minimum income or benefit payment – did I get you right at the beginning that your country used to be called the Gold Coast?"

"Yes, Mr President; that is the name bestowed on it by the Europeans."

"My guess is that your land abounds in gold; otherwise the idea would not have occurred to the Europeans to bestow that name on the country, would they?"

"Mr President, you are right. There is still quite a good deal of gold mining taking place there."

"If that is the case, why have you travelled all the way to the US to seek help? Citizens of a country abounding in gold coming to beg the US for help? Good Lord, please restrain the mouth of the Donald so he doesn't say anything that will be considered disparaging or derogatory by his nice visitors from Ghana!"

"Mr President, our country is indeed blessed with various minerals – gold, diamonds, bauxite, manganese. To top it all, in 2010 substantial finds of oil were discovered. Unfortunately, common residents like ourselves never benefit from such resources."

"That is bad; really grim. Your leaders need frank talk; real frank chatting. They cannot dwell in luxurious villas and drive expensive cars and leave the rest of the populace to dwell in absolute misery."

"Mr President, can you please do us a favour?"

"Don't mention money! The Donald does not dish out cash – hard-earned cash for no reason. He is not a charity!"

"Please keep your money, Mr President. What I am requesting from you is simply to tell this fact to the face of each African president you meet in future, telling them to take care of their citizens and not leave them alone to wallow in abject poverty."

"Of course, I will do exactly that. As you already hinted, I believe in frank talk. If I don't like you, I say it to your face! I don't wait until you are away before passing derogatory comments behind your back. I am not like Obama! You surely have heard about Obama, haven't you?

"I have, Mr President."

"You may recall that early in his presidency he travelled to Ghana – have I said it right? – and made a very nice and polished speech to those corrupt politicians in Africa. Instead of naming each one of them and shaming them, he just talked around and around the issue. What effect did that nice speech have on them? Nothing, absolutely nothing. The bribery, corruption, nepotism and what-have-you persisted. Yes, I understand things have got worse. That is obvious otherwise what would have prompted you to embark on your long journey?

"If ever I meet them, African leaders, under the same roof, the Donald will expose their corrupt practices one by one; by the time he finishes his speech, hardly anyone will be left in the room! Indeed, I will call them one by one by name and point out their corrupt practices to them – in front of the world press.

"A good many of them, indeed, are hiding considerable wealth in the US and other Western countries; meanwhile ordinary folks like yourselves continue to wallow in poverty. Bad, very bad people!"

"Mr President, if you are aware of such monies, then why do you not use your authority to help repatriate those funds back to where they belong?"

"Friends, the rules are not that simple. If, for example, I used executive powers to enact a law, they will appeal the case. And be sure of this: our so-called judges will rule againſt me, accusing me of infringing on banking confidentiality rules and regulations. It is outrageous, but the thieves are taking advantage of such provisions in our legal syſtem to commit criminal activities." He paused for a while, probably to judge our response. He continued when nothing was forthcoming.

"The interference of our judges – sometimes I find it beyond belief. You surely muſt have heard about 9/11. Well, juſt to recap. On that day, on September 11, 2001, a group of Muslim zealots flew planes into the twin towers of the New York World Trade Center. That terroriſt act led to the death of thousands.

"On assumption of power, I decided to ban Muslims from some parts of the globe from entering our country. I was juſt saying: 'Folks, ſtay where you are and don't come over to diſturb our peace.' Their religion preaches an eye for an eye. The Donald was doing nothing apart from following on the teachings of their Koran – to pay them on their own terms, an eye for an eye.

"As far as I am concerned, it amounted to simple logic. They hit us hard, so I decided to hit back. Lo and behold! The so-called human rights activiſts of the country found fault with the Donald!

"'Why are you behaving in such a manner, Mr President? That is againſt their human rights!' What about the human rights of those who perished in the demonic attack, my friends? In the end our so-called judges supported them and prevented me from paying them an eye for an eye."

At that juncture he took a look at his watch.

"Friends, our time is very limited, so let us move on.

"Why are you singling out the US for help? You could juſt as well have contacted the Europeans."

"We have done juſt that, Mr President. We have been to Berlin, Brussels and London."

"Who did you meet in Berlin, Angelika Merkel?"

"Yes, Mr President?"

"Did she promise to help?"

"She only made vague promises."

"The Germans, forget them! They are penny pinchers."

"Pardon me, Mr President. English is not our first language so please be simple. May I ask you what you mean by 'penny pincher'?"

"Oh, I thought you understood. Anyway, I just wanted to say that they don't easily part with their money. That is not by any means speaking ill of them. That is the fact. Indeed, I have over the years demanded that they contribute their fair share towards the NATO budget – to no avail!

"They want to sell their big cars – Mercedes, BMW, VW – you can go on naming them – in the US. But they don't want to contribute to their defence. Out of exasperation I decided to impose tariffs on their vehicles; now I bet they will begin to shout foul!"

He paused to gauge our reaction, then continued after a while.

"So, you got only vague promises in Berlin? What happened in Brussels and London?"

"The same empty promises, Mr President!"

"Well, that is the reality of the world we live in. Everyone for himself and God for us all. I wonder why people have issues with the Donald for his 'America First!' stance."

"Mr President, I also have issues with that."

"What is wrong with that folks?"

"We would have wished you would declare instead 'Human Beings First!', for, at the end of the day, we are all bound by our common humanity."

"Before I comment on that, I'd like to ask you a question."

"Please go ahead, Mr President."

"I guess all of you have children, right?"

"Yes, that is the case."

"Now If you wake up in the morning, who do you think first about, your own children or your neighbours' children?"

"My children, Mr President."

"Well, you have answered the question! Why then are you raising an issue with my 'America First' policy?"

"With all due respect, Mr President, I must disagree with you on the matter."

"Why?"

"The comparison is not appropriate. Whereas it is indeed legitimate for you to consider your own children ahead of those of others, in my view it is a different matter when it comes to the general issue of world politics."

"I don't see it that way. It was the people of America who voted me to power; those are the folk I need to cater for first."

"In my view, there is no need for such a statement, for when it comes to the standard of living you Americans are playing in the premier league with other nations like Germany, the UK, France, etc. We, on the other hand, are playing in the bottom-most league!

"Indeed, Mr President, when I first set foot in your country, I thought I had landed in heaven instead of a country on Earth. Your beautiful cities, wonderful houses, excellent road network, your posh cars on your well-maintained roads... The people we saw on the streets seem very well fed, too. Everything abounds in your shops that are really impressive. So, Mr President, wherein lies our problem? Why do you create the impression as if dooms-day is knocking on the doors of the beautiful American dream?"

"So let me see if I understand this correctly", the president said, "you want me to open the gates of our country and let in the millions of destitute of the world?" He shook his head. "No, we cannot afford to do that! It is my duty, as the commander in chief of our armed forces, to defend our precious country from such an invasion!

145

"But to get back to the issue of poverty, want and suffering in your part of the world. Allow me to draw an allegory to my own life. I don't know whether others have spread false news about my personal wealth. I am not trying to blow my trumpet before the whole world, but the fact remains that I *am* wealthy. Indeed, I am a billionaire. I did not receive my billions on a silver platter. No, my billions were not handed down to me on a silver platter. I earned it the very hard way.

"On a few occasions, I was threatened with bankruptcy. Instead of giving up in despair, or resigning to fate, I chose instead to fight on.

"You people in Africa need to develop a similar mindset, or attitude. You must sit down and think, think, think, about ways and means of solving your problems, instead of waiting on others to do so for you.

"The other day I was watching a documentary on Africa on Fox News. I was really disgusted to see human beings crawling on all fours on the streets of a major city in Africa – I don't remember exactly the name of the country concerned.

"I asked myself: 'Where are the political leaders of the country? Why cannot the authorities erect homes to house such disadvantaged individuals of society?' This is not a big deal at all. Surely it won't require a great deal of effort to create such facility! Or do you expect the Americans to come down to get the job done?

"My goodness, what is going on in Africa! Well, I'd better keep my mouth shut or the fake press will tomorrow spread false news to the effect I resorted to derogatory terms to describe Africa.

"Concerning that particular instance that everyone has been referring to, I don't really recall using the term attributed to me."

"May I please know what Mr President is driving at?"

"Oh, it seems you have not heard the accusation against me. Never mind – you surely have much more pressings needs to attend to in your little village to be occupied with such whimsical rumours spread by the fake news press about me."

"You are right, Mr President, we are so preoccupied with the challenges of everyday life that we hardly have the time or energy to follow everything that happens in the world."

"Yet another issue I want to raise with you", the president resumed. "The other day I was watching TV. I don't remember which channel – definitely not CNN... I don't watch CNN, its full of fake news – but let me continue where I left off ... Oh, pardon me, I forgot where I left off..."

"Mr President, I think you wanted to speak about something you saw on TV!"

"Oh, yeah! I remember. Yes, it was about the poor canalisation in one of the major cities of Africa. The condition has prevailed for decades, it was reported. The situation has worsened of late because of the citizens throwing litter into the open gutters to clog them and make an already bad situation worse. More than 20 years after the problem was identified, it has still not been resolved!

"I asked myself, why can't they get the problem fixed? Surely there are loads of young men and women roaming the streets. Why don't the authorities employ them to clean the gutters and eventually cover them? This does not require input of foreign capital to achieve, does it?

"I could lecture you the whole day about the petty things you people could do yourselves to get your economy moving. Well, the Donald is a busy individual, so cannot find that much time for you.

"You touched on the rich resources of your country. What in God's name is happening with all those resources – oil, gold, diamonds, uranium, cobalt, fertile soil, etc.? Wallowing

147

in absolute poverty in the face of abundant natural resources! My goodness!" He paused. "I am really enjoying your presence. Unfortunately, however, I have a very busy schedule. Soon I'll be called for another engagement.

"Before we part however, I want to propose a deal. I am indeed known for my deals. It is not for nought that people call me 'the deal-maker president'. They have in fact always called me the deal-maker. I don't make deals for the sake of making them. I am known instead for making only good sound deals; that explains how I have made my billions.

"I am not unaware of some of the challenges prevailing in Africa by dint of its location in a hot tropical climate. For example, parasites and germs that bring diseases such as malaria, Ebola, sleeping sickness, etc., thrive in your climate. Poisonous creatures like snakes and scorpions also pose a hazard to the human dwellers; lack of rain can also easily lead to drought and famine.

"Notwithstanding the prevailing natural challenges, I will request the US Congress for permission – you also have to seek the approval of your leaders – for what I term a 'continental swap'! I am indeed proposing that we swap your African continent with our country."

"What do you mean by that, Mr President?"

"One might in actual fact refer to it as a country/continent swap. What it entails is the following:

"Human beings on our respective continents will vacate their homes and their properties; they will be permitted to take along the barest necessities in the form of clothes and personal hygiene needed for about a week. Everything on the surface of present-day America will be taken over by the Africans. We on the other hand, will move and occupy Africa.

"I agree that we will be taking over a land surface larger than that of our country. In my opinion, it is nevertheless a good deal

for the inequality in the surface mass of our respective countries (or continents), which will be compensated by the material wealth we have produced on our continent. I have in mind,
among others, the infrastructure, the good cities, the technological advancement, etc." He leaned back in his chair. "Yes, give
me Africa, and come and take our land. We will give you whatever you find here – the highways, the highly developed infrastructure, everything. But be warned, my friends, if you fail to
take proper care of what we are bequeathing to you, if you mess
up things, do not call on us in our beautiful Unites States of New
Africa and beg us to come back and put things right for you. It
is a done deal, okay! Only subject to the approval of Congress. I
am confident they will approve it – for sure they will."

We were so much taken aback by his proposal that, at first,
we were lost for words. After the initial shock, Douglas as usual
spoke on our behalf.

"Mr President", he began, "is it real news we are hearing
from your mouth, or are you perhaps quoting fake news, origi-
nating from the likes of CNN, NYT, WP, etc.?"

"This is real news; no fake news", the president grinned.
"Indeed, you are hearing it from the horse's own mouth. Subject
to Congressional approval – and I will surely apply my influence
on the House and Senate to approve the measure – I am certain the Republican-controlled House will approve the measure.
I only need to convince the Democrats to come on board – but
I'm sure they will agree.

"Indeed, taking over Africa with its huge reserves of minerals of all kinds, its vast agricultural potential, is something that
should appeal to many business-minded folks. We only need to
put measures in place to contain some of the natural hazards I
touched upon earlier. I'm confident our brilliant scientists will be
up to the challenge. We could set up vast solar parks and stations

on the Sahara. Yes, we will utilise the huge solar potential of the Sahara for our common interest."

"Mr President", Douglas interrupted, "before we forget. We just want to draw your attention to the Poverty March that is scheduled to take place in New York the day after tomorrow."

"Oh, I heard about that on Fox News. What has that got to do with yourselves?"

"The march came about through our initiative."

"Hey, my friends form little Mpintimpi, do you want to turn the world upside down?"

"Mr President, it has nothing to do with turning the world upside down! It is matter of drawing the attention of the world to the harsh living conditions of ourselves and millions of others living in abject poverty. I want at this stage, Mr President, to politely put this question to you. Have you in all your life ever experienced hunger?"

"Hunger? No, never! My parents spoke about times, long before they got to know each other, when each of them had to struggle to make ends meet. Even then, their daily meals were assured. Thanks to the hard work of my parents, and later *my* hard work, I have never, I repeat, *never* known want in my life."

"So, Mr President, you have no idea of hunger. We and millions of others have known and continue to experience hunger. Indeed, just as we are speaking, millions of people somewhere on the planet are going about with empty stomachs while others are retiring to bed hungry.

"The idea of the Poverty March came about during our stay in London. It is taking place the day after tomorrow. The cardinal demand of the march will be a call for a legally binding daily income or benefit payment of one dollar and fifty cents per head for any resident of planet Earth independent of where he or she happens to reside.

"We shall publish a 10-point action plan outlining the proposals we are presenting to the world as to how the proposed benefit scheme can be financed. We hope we can count on your support, Mr President."

"I am of course happy to support you, as long as it does not conflict with my America First agenda!"

"Mr President, I hear you are a believer."

"Indeed I am."

"Let me put a question to you: if Almighty God looks down from above onto Earth, what does he see first, America or the world?"

"Hey, my friend from Africa, why are you comparing me to God Almighty? I am an ordinary human being, the President of the US, so I see only America when I wake up from bed, so I am right to hold on to my America First policy, am I not?"

At this juncture he consulted his watch.

"Come, on, friends", said he, "Get up and follow me, I want to show you a bit of the White House. Usually, I delegate the job to a subordinate, but somehow I'm beginning to fall in love with you. You see, other accuse me of being racist. I am not! To be honest with you, I get on well with everyone. The Donald does not have a racist bone in him, that is a fact!"

We were pleasantly surprised at the kindness meted out to us by the president; it was beyond what any of us could have imagined.

As he saw the awe in our faces while he showed us the magnificent corridors, rooms and halls of the historical building, he suddenly stopped. Looking at the four of us, he began:

"I can read from your faces that you are enjoying the viewing. Others may want to conceal one historical aspect of the White House from you. That however is not how the Donald operates. I will be frank and open with you. In some respects this building owes you people a debt of gratitude."

151

"A debt of gratitude? What do you mean by that, Mr President?"

"By virtue of the fact that it was built with slave labour; with slaves from your part of the world – they may very well have been your relatives, who knows?"

"Mr President, that then is a good reason why you should support our mission!" Douglas remarked.

"But you were not directly involved in the construction! If anything, it is the African-American population, the direct descendants of the of slaves who could raise such an issue, not yourselves!"

"Mr President, in my view we also deserve compensation. The slave trade depleted our continent of a good proportion of our well-built men and women. The strong and able-bodied ones deemed capable of making the treacherous journey were selected, while the weak and disable were left behind."

"Well, my good friends, we better leave this explosive theme for now." He continued: "Just to give you a brief history of the building... Construction work begun on 13 October 1792. On 1 November 1800, President John Adams became the first president to move into the newly-built premises. The building did not receive its present official name until 1901."

After spending about 20 minutes taking us around, he took us back to his office.

Not long after we had taken our seats, one of his aides signalled to him that our time was up.

"Well, I'm afraid we have to part company", the president said. "I have taken note of what you told me. I will present my proposal to Congress as already indicated. As I await the outcome of the deliberations of my continent–country swap proposal, I will urge Congress to release some funds to help establish a poultry farm in your village. Do take good care of it, folks!"

"Mr President, we are thankful to you for the remarkable kindness you have shown us. Indeed, contrary to how others have portrayed you, we have experienced you as a sympathetic, big-hearted and down-to-earth individual.

"We have decided to reciprocate your kindness by extending an invitation to you to visit our little village. Yes indeed, on behalf of the residents of Mpintimpi, we hereby cordially extend our warmest invitation to you to visit our humble village of Mpintimpi."

"You are inviting me to visit your village?"

"Yes indeed."

"Hey, Melania", he called to the First Lady, "come and listen to this yourself! We have been invited to visit Mpiiiin…"

"Mpintimpi", Douglas helped him out.

"I better mind my words; otherwise I could be accused of disrespect for our friends from Africa. The next thing we know, CNN and the others will have picked on it and made fake news out of it!

"Seriously, Melania", he said to the First Lady, "can we feel comfortable, even in their capital Accra? Let alone in Mpintimpi?"

"You remember I was in Accra recently", she replied. "I enjoyed my stay. As for the little village, I have no idea. Well, they are human like ourselves, after all. If they are able to survive there, why not ourselves?"

"Well, even though I would like to visit, for practical reasons, I don't think it can go ahead. There surely is no suitable landing place for the presidential helicopter."

"And the beast?"

"I don't think the FBI people will permit us to drive the distance from Accra to the village with the amazing presidential beast."

Turning to us he said:

"I am not going to turn down your invitation outright. I will pass it on to our chief of staff and see what he comes up with!" Shortly thereafter we parted company with the presidential couple.

***

The idea of the US/Africa swap proposed by the president made headlines over the next few days. Heated debates and discussions on the matter took place on radio, TV, as well as on various social media platforms.

Whereas others dismissed it as crazy, out of the blue, unworkable, etc., others thought it was something worth considering.

To quote one far-right newspaper in a country whose name I am withholding:

"If ever we embark on the swap, the lazy Africans will surely mess things up! Mark it on the wall – it will be only a matter of time when they line up on the borders of the New Africa pleading with us to let them in!!"

Other papers took a more moderate tone: "Let's just go down and build the infrastructure for them – roads, rail networks, airports, solar parks, hospitals, schools, homes, etc., and leave the place for them so they can just feel comfortable and so do not find the need to embark on treacherous journeys over the Sahara and the Mediterranean in their attempt to reach Europe. It is up to the Africans to take good care of their own countries; if they don't, they would have no one but themselves to blame."

14

We demand ploughshares and not swords!

The preparations for the global meeting of the poor and down-trodden that had been going on for a while were nearing their climax.

Owing to the huge logistics involved in the organisation of the event, we delegated part of the task to volunteers from various groups, movements and organisations – human rights activists, environmentalists, anti-capitalists, etc.

To finance the work of the organising committee, an online crowdfunding appeal had been launched. It had in the meantime raked in a hundred thousand US dollars.

We kept in close touch with the organising committee throughout.

The global gathering of the poor was to last three days. Delegates from all over the globe were expected to arrive in New York on the eve of the occasion. The formal opening would be on Friday.

After the opening ceremony, and speeches from selected delegates, the meeting was to break up into four groups.

They would report back on the next day, Saturday, for plenum discussions on various themes. A 10-point action plan would be adopted in the course of the evening.

The next day, Sunday, delegates would gather at the UN headquarters building at 10am for the Global Poverty March. Starting from the headquarters building, it would follow a route approved by the street authorities and end at Central Park. There, the 10-point action plan would be formally presented to the rest of the world.

At the same time as the main march in New York, similar marches would take place in major cities throughout the world – Accra, Amsterdam, Berlin, Brussels, Jerusalem, London, Los Angeles, Mexico City, Moscow, Paris, Sydney, Tokyo, Toronto – you can go on naming them!

The plan was for those cities with the necessary facilities to link up directly with New York via satellite to follow the closing speech. Where that was not possible, a copy of the speech would be read out to them.

At our request, an emergency meeting of the UN Security Council had been called for the eve of the conference. The four-member delegation would appear before the council to discuss our concerns and demands.

Prior to the meeting of the Security Council in the afternoon, a meeting with the secretary general had been arranged.

The short flight from Washington DC to New York was uneventful. We checked in at a budget hotel on the outskirts of the huge metropolis.

We arrived at the UN headquarters, located in the Turtle Bay neighbourhood of Manhattan, in good time on Thursday morning for the meeting with the secretary-general, which was scheduled for 10am. The extraordinary meeting of the UN Security Council was to follow four hours later.

***

The UN secretary-general, Mr António Guterres, welcomed us wholeheartedly into his imposing office. After the exchange of cordial greetings, Douglas got straight down to business.:

"Mr Secretary-General, we deem it an honour, indeed a great pleasure to meet you today", he began. "We appreciate the important role the UN is playing in the world towards maintaining peace and understanding among the peoples of the world. As I researched the role of the UN in the world prior to this meeting, several issues that were unknown to us came to light. Among others we learnt about the World Food Programme, set up by the UN to provides food and assistance to those in need. It was said that some 91 million people in 83 countries have so far benefitted from the programme.

"I also read about the UN's sustainable development goals for 2030. After reading, we began to ask ourselves – is this a fairy tale or reality? I would like to invite you to our little village to see things at first hand, the harsh living conditions we are exposed to every day. I am not saying we are starving, but things are tough!

"We are calling for the UN to ensure that universal human rights, as set out in the Universal Human Rights Convention as enshrined in the UN Charter, are upheld also in our little village. We did not set the rules, they were set by the UN, so we expect the UN to enforce them.

"We are not prepared to wait for years for the enforcement of something which, in our opinion, can be achieved tomorrow.

"As I listened to the radio the other day, I heard that in one of the rich countries of the world 30% of food produced or purchased goes to waste! That goes to show we are in a position of solving the problem of hunger right now – it is only a matter distribution/redistribution of resources.

"We, the poor of this world, are demanding a fair share of the resources of this world. We are not advocating a forceful revolution, certainly not a bloody revolution. No, we are just demanding that the UN should implement its own resolutions.

"Over the next three days, we are going to deliberate and bring up solutions to our problems. Over the years intellectuals have been made to plan for us. We demand that, in future, if the UN wants to help the poor in |Ghana and elsewhere, they send delegates to talk to the people directly involved and not to our politicians and bureaucrats in capitals such as Accra, Lagos, Manila and elsewhere.

"Sir, we don't trust our leaders. I am not saying they are all the same; unfortunately, a good proportion of them are selfish and self-seeking, a body of individuals who care only for themselves and their families.

"I want to narrate a story to strengthen my point. A friend of mine was sent to do his national service in a village. Through his own initiative, he got funds meant for the handicapped, which until then had not been claimed or released from the responsible department in the capital Accra. Before the money could be paid to the beneficiaries, however, it had to be signed off by a district chief executive. When he approached him for the signature, the district chief executive told him bluntly that unless he got his share of the money he was not going to sign! That, Mr Secretary-General, could be the calibre of government officials through whose hands funds from the UN meant for the poor could pass," Douglas shook his head with a deep sigh.

"I have taken note of the points raised", began Mr Guterres. "You will agree with me that the UN cannot be at every place at the same time. Often, we have no choice than to work with whatever personnel the beneficiary country places at our disposal.

"Much as we would wish to help everyone, our means are limited. We can do as much as member states place at our disposal. Often, we have to get on our knees and beg member states to place the required means at our disposal. Under such circumstance we have no choice but to prioritise.

"I have no doubt that life at your end is harsh. Well, you may not believe me, but there are some who are living under more harsh conditions than yourselves. I have in mind civilians presently trapped in conflict areas in Syria, Yemen, Myanmar, etc. It is a bitter world, my friends."

"We agree with you, Mr Secretary-General, that the UN is doing what it can to help alleviate suffering in the world. Nevertheless, as we mentioned earlier on, we are not benefiting from any such ventures. Indeed, we feel neglected by the world community.

"The saying has it that a hungry man is an angry man. I have come up with a modified version of that saying – a hungry person, yes someone threatened with starvation, is full of ideas, sometimes radical, as to how to end his or her hunger. In keeping with that thinking, we have come up with ideas as to how the world community can help end abject poverty.

"We shall publish our ideas and plans at the end of the summit. You, as well as the various UN institutions, will be served copies.

"The UN is doing great! In all our efforts we will regard the UN as a partner and not as a competitor or opponent."

***

We arrived at the appointed time for our meeting with the UN Security Council.

Present at the meeting were representatives from the five permanent members of the council, in alphabetical order – China, France, the Russian Federation, the UK, the US.

Also in attendance were the ten non-permanent members at the time. These were – Bolivia, Côte d'Ivoire, Equatorial

Guinea, Ethiopia, Kazakhstan, Kuwait, Netherlands, Peru, Poland and Sweden.

After the initial greetings and introduction, we were given the opportunity to present our case:

As usual, Douglas spoke on our behalf. The following is the full text of his speech:

"Ladies and Gentlemen of the UN Security Council,

"On behalf of the executive and millions of members of the Poverty Crusaders Movement, I send you warm greetings.

"Ladies and gentlemen, I consider it a great privilege to be given the opportunity to address the UN Security Council today.

"Before I proceed, I want to take this opportunity to express my sincere thanks to the Secretary-General, for not only arranging this meeting, but also placing the premises of the UN at our disposal for our meeting.

"Over the next three days, representatives of the poor and deprived of our common planet, will converge on New York.

"For the first time ever, representatives from the poor and deprived of the world, if only for a brief period of time, will take over the whole UN complex to deliberate on ways and means to end global poverty.

"Before I proceed further, please permit me, ladies and gentlemen, to refresh your minds concerning the provisions of Articles 25 and 26 of the United Nations Universal Declaration of Human Rights 1948.

Article 25
'1. Everyone has the right to a standard of living adequate for the health and well-being of himself and of his family, including food, clothing, housing and medical care and necessary social services, and the right to security in the event of

unemployment, sickness, disability, widowhood, old age or other lack of livelihood in circumstances beyond his control.
'2. Motherhood and childhood are entitled to special care and assistance. All children, whether born in or out of wedlock, shall enjoy the same social protection.

Article 26
'1. Everyone has the right to education. Education shall be free, at least in the elementary and fundamental stages. Elementary education shall be compulsory. Technical and professional education shall be made generally available and higher education shall be equally accessible to all on the basis of merit.
'2. Education shall be directed to the full development of the human personality and to the strengthening of respect for human rights and fundamental freedoms. It shall promote understanding, tolerance and friendship among all nations, racial or religious groups, and shall further the activities of the United Nations for the maintenance of peace.
'3. Parents have a prior right to choose the kind of education that shall be given to their children.'

"Much as the UN has over the years dedicated resources and manpower towards poverty alleviation, in our opinion, – you may disagree – the effort of the UN can be described as a drop in a vast ocean mass.

"Whoever does not agree with me on that issue is invited to come with me on a tour of various slum settlements spread throughout the world.

"Ladies and gentlemen, so long as millions, yes, a considerable proportion of the world population, dwell in abject poverty, the UN's set goal of maintaining peace on Earth will be elusive, for poverty and lack of perspective often serve as a breeding ground for conflicts of various types.

"Everyone has the right to a standard of living adequate for the health and well-being of himself and of his family, including food, clothing, housing and medical care and necessary social services, and the right to security in the event of unemployment, sickness, disability, widowhood, old age or other lack of livelihood in circumstances beyond his control.

"The statistics point in a very different direction, ladies and gentlemen.

"I found out in my research online that, just as we are speaking, nearly half of the world's population, – more than 3 billion people – live on less than \$2.50 a day. Another 1.3 billion live in extreme poverty – less than \$1.25 a day. The case of over 805 million people worldwide is even more precarious – they have not enough to eat.

"In the face of such stark statistics, the question that we need to ask ourselves is – has the world got enough stocks of food to feed everyone?

"The experts no doubt agree on this. Why then should some go to bed hungry when there is abundant food to go around?

"Has the world gotten enough resources and know-how to provide clean drinking water for everyone? The answer in our opinion is a big *yes*. The reality however is that that is not the case.

"Everyone has the right to basic health care; has the world adequate resources to maintain the basics? Yes, we believe we have.

"Everyone has the right to affordable housing. Has the world not got enough raw materials to produce basic homes for everyone? I certainly believe, with the will and the needed effort, humankind is capable of doing exactly that. Yes, we can!

"Ladies and gentlemen of the Security Council, since it is the UN that came up with the Universal Declaration of Human Rights, we are demanding that the UN takes steps to ensure the very minimum requirements of the declaration are upheld.

"I recently came across figures on how much money countries spend on arms – a fact that sends the blood boiling in me.

"Time will not permit me to dwell on the details. To sum up, the figures had it that every year countries, yes, all member states of the UN, an organisation that has made working towards world peace its cardinal goal, spend trillions on weapons.

"We accept the fact that we don't live in an ideal world; but rather dwell in an unstable world. Still, in our view, nations can radically reduce their defence spending without compromising on their security. The money set free could be used to support the poor.

"The Poverty Crusaders movement has come up with a 10-point action plan offering solutions to some of the problems touched upon, including the issue of the global arms trade. I do not want to reveal the plan today. It will be published in due course. We will serve every country a copy. Thank you very much for your time."

Judging from the reaction of those present, the speech received a mixed reaction, with some present applauding, whilst others sat still.

"Thank you very much for your contribution", said the President of the Council. "We shall await your 10-point plan. We shall deliberate on them during our next meeting. Should we pass any resolution after studying and debating them, such a resolution will be published in the usual manner. Whatever the case, we shall communicate the outcome of our deliberations with you.

"May I now please ask our honoured visitors to leave the hall as we move on to the next agenda for the day."

The President got out of his seat, accompanied us to the exit and bade us a polite goodbye. Moments later we were back on the busy streets of New York.

15

United Nations summit extraordinaire – Day 1

The day of the Poverty Crusaders conference finally dawned. From all over the world, the poor, the destitute, the underprivileged descended on the UN premises in New York.

To report on the historic occasion, the world's media had descended on the city nicknamed "The City that Never Sleeps". Hoisted on transmitter vans were huge satellite bowls bearing the inscriptions of world-renowned media outlets, the likes of ABC, BBC, CNN, Fox.

Reporters from the print media were also well represented – *New York Times, Washington Post, Herald Tribune*, to mention a few.

For once the attention of the world's press was focussed on the deprived and neglected of the world.

Finally, the Poverty Crusaders conference got underway in the plenum of the General Assembly building of the UN.

Delegates came from slums, shanty towns, ghettos, squalid settlements and whatever other terms there are for dilapidated, run-down, ramshackle areas, unfit for human habitation, types of communities that exist throughout the world.

For the sake of brevity, only the names of a selected few of the ramshackle human settlements from which the participants came are listed here:

* Agbogbloshie, Accra, Ghana.
* Kibera slum, Nairobi, Kenya.
* Khayelitsha slum, Cape Town, South Africa.
* Makoko, Lagos, Nigeria.
* Orangi Town, Karachi, Pakistan.
* Dharavi, Mumbai, India.
* Manila North Cemetery slum, Manila, the Philippines.
* Ciudad Nez, Mexico City, Mexico.
* Cité Soleil, Port-au-Prince, Haiti.
* Mahwa Aser, Sanaa, Yemen.

***

Though the gathering was a result of our initiative, we did not want to create the impression that everything revolved around us. We therefore decided to select someone else, apart from ourselves, to chair the meeting. A day prior to the opening, leaders from the participating groups met to choose from six candidates. In the end, they decided on a 40-year-old woman, Mrs Rosamie Ocampo, a delegate from the Philippines, a resident of one of the Manila Cemetery slums.

***

At exactly 8:30am, on Friday, 22 June 2018, Mrs Rosamie Ocampo took to the stage to formally declare the extraordinary summit at the UN headquarters open.

Below is a short excerpt from her speech:

"Ladies and Gentlemen, I want to take the opportunity to bid you a warm welcome to this historic meeting. Over the next three days, we shall occupy ourselves with our problems and come up with ideas as to how to end our misery.

"Often when I ponder over our plight, I compare our situation to a person caught between a rock and a hard place. On the one hand the unfavourable polices of the rich industrialised countries towards the so-called third-world countries where the majority of us live contribute to the impoverishment of such countries.

"The ruling elite of our countries, on their part, keep for themselves the very little by way of resources left, leaving us to go empty handed.

"After the policies and practices of the powers that be have led us to wallow in absolute poverty, others take advantage of us to feed their greed and satisfy their curiosity as the case may be.

"I am referring here to slum tourism. In the North Manila Cemetery slum where I grew up, for example, the practice is booming.

"My dear friends, what kind of world do we live in? A world that permits others to dwell in misery only for others, mostly rich overseas tourists, to pay money to have a look at the misery of their fellow humans?

"Has society come to accept slums so much as a normal way of life, that there is nothing that can be done to do away with such squalid, appalling, dilapidated settlements everywhere in the world?

"Ladies and gentlemen, I have a different view on the matter. Over the next three days let us come up with ideas to show the world that it is indeed possible to rid the world of abject poverty.

"I want at this stage to invite Mr Douglas Akwasi Abankwah from the tiny village Mpintimpi in Ghana to deliver the opening address."

Amid thunderous applause, Douglas, simply dressed in a T-shirt and a worn-out pair of jeans we had acquired for him from a second-hand shop the previous day, mounted the podium:

"Ladies and Gentlemen,

167

"On behalf of the residents of Mpintimpi and the other three members of our delegation, I want to welcome you all to this auguſt meeting. When we set out from our little village in Ghana to present our humble petition to our president, hardly could we have imagined that that action would lead to a global movement!

"We are not claiming the glory for ourselves alone; the glory belongs to all assembled here together with the over one billion poor we represent.

"We, the poor and deprived, feel abandoned from all sides.

"The ruling elite of our various countries – whether they were democratically elected or got to power by means of the gun or inheritance – all seem more intereſted in their own welfare than the plight of the poor in their respective countries.

"Not only have the politicians of our respective countries let us down, the rich and influential countries of the developed world as well as multinational organisations or inſtitutions – the World Bank, the IMF, the big multinational corporations, etc. – have likewise let us down.

"Those countries of the developed world – they may call it legitimate – regard their citizens firſt. But where does that lead us?

"Well, to answer that queſtion and propose solutions to global poverty, is the goal of this meeting.

"Over the next three days, we shall deliberate over the issues, both in the general assembly, and in working groups. At the end of the three days we shall come up with our demands to the world – to develop solutions to the problem of world poverty, solutions that are workable from our own perspective.

"Indeed, up till now, the task of finding solutions to the problems of the world has been entruſted to people who have themselves never known poverty!

"I am not implying that only those who have known personal poverty and deprivation are capable of devising the right ſtrategies to alleviate it. No, that is not what I am driving at.

"Still, I often ask myself, how can one expect, for example, a president who grew up in affluence; a successful businessman, a billionaire who has not known poverty, to really understand the concerns of the poor and deprived?

"Whereas, it is possible for such an individual to develop strategies towards fighting poverty, in my opinion it is only those who themselves have tasted poverty who can adequately tackle it. We have met, ladies and gentlemen, to deliberate on the problems of this world, to find solutions to our problems, indeed to tackle the problems besetting us, from our own perspective.

"We should not only come up with proposals aimed at ending abject poverty; we should also show the world how resources required to implement our proposals can be derived.

"Ladies and gentlemen, this is our time, this is our opportunity – let us not let it slip by; no, let us seize it to our advantage. Thank you very much for your time."

The speech was greeted with a standing ovation.

After calm had returned to the plenum, the chairwoman took the stage a second time:

"Thank you very much Mr Abankwah. As we heard from his speech, we are going to deliberate on the problems of this world, with the goal of finding solutions for them, from our own perspective.

"Towards this end we have divided the world into six zones. There is no doubt that Africa, Asia and South America bear the greatest brunt of poverty; consequently, we have allocated two working groups to each of the regions.

"One group each will be formed by Europe, North America, Australia and New Zealand – bringing the number to ten.

"Each group has been given a theme. They are to discuss, or deliberate, on the allocated theme. The goal is to develop a 10-point action plan.

"They will report to the plenum tomorrow. After further discussion, a final 10-point action plan will be put forward.

"The meeting will come to a close on the third day with the final communique.

"Before we depart into our working groups, a representative from some of the global regions will deliver short introductory speeches to the plenum. We shall begin with Africa."

***

At that stage a female delegate, still in her teens, got up from her seat and headed for the podium. The plenum erupted into a spontaneous applause as she walked towards the podium.

"Good morning, ladies and gentlemen.

"I bring you warm greeting s from the Kayayo Association of Kumasi, Ghana.

"The term *Kayayo* will almost certainly be Latin in the ears of many of you, so I shall provide a short explanation.

"It refers to head porters, who, like myself, are mostly female, who carry loads on their heads from one point to another in towns and cities in my country for a fee.

"I am aged 15. I am not the youngest *Kayayo* around. Indeed, there are children as young as six years engaged in the trade!!

"I am the fifth of six of my mother's children. When I was six years old, my father passed away under tragic circumstances. He developed abdominal pains and was taken to hospital. When we got to the hospital, we were told the hospital was operating on a 'pay as you go' basis. Unable to pay the fee demanded on the spot, father was not attended to.

"We had no choice then but to send him back home. Mother went around looking for a loan. By the time she got someone to lend her the required amount, Father's condition had deteriorated considerably. He passed away at the gates of the hospital.

"Unable to pay our fees following Father's passing away, I had to stop going to school. Not only did I stop attending school, I had to join Mother in her daily tedious job as a head porter. I have since been in the business for nine years.

"Often, I ask myself – what will become of me in my old age when I am no longer in a position to carry loads around for a living?

"It is in the light of this that I am particularly enthralled by idea of a global benefit system that will cater for those who, through no fault of theirs, are unable to cater for themselves.

"Ladies and gentlemen, we should not rest on our laurels but rather maintain the momentum in our fight for the rights of the poor and downtrodden. Thank you very much for your time."

***

Next on the list was a delegate from North America. After the usual greetings, he began:

"We are ruled by the political elite. Because they are well fed, clothed and housed, in my opinion, they are not doing much to tackle the huge problems facing the poor in general and we slum residents in particular.

"In several places in the world, governments have left the task of caring for those who fall through the social net to extended family members. In many instances such individuals themselves are struggling to make ends meet. How can the poor care for the poor?

"In some instances, charitable organisations step in to offer assistance. While admiring the great job being done by such organisations, the bottom line is: It is governments that have the first responsibility for the well-being of their citizens. Yet, in many parts of the world, they are shunning that responsibility.

"Ladies and gentlemen, let us send a message to our corrupt leaders that we are not going to take it any longer!"

***

South America was next:

"There has so far been talk of international efforts to eradicate poverty. Ladies and gentlemen, I am past 70 years. Disease has rendered me incapable of working for the last ten years. So far, I have not received help from any quarter, national or international. The question that I ask myself is – where has all the help gone to?

"I am told that on a regular basis, the UN holds conferences to adopt plans towards poverty eradication.

"I ask myself – why don't such conferences invite us, yes, we who are directly affected by poverty, and offer us the opportunity to contribute to their deliberations?

"But no, instead, during such conferences, participants, individuals, many of whom have no idea what it is to be poor, no idea how to live with practically nothing, seek to find solutions to our problems.

"The UN is said to have set out a target to eradicate much of global poverty by 2030. Friends, I know with all certainty that I won't be around in the year 2030.

"I am calling for immediate action on the matter. Yes, I am calling for the introduction of a global welfare state system to cater for the poor.

"Some will argue that such hand-outs will render us lazy. I don't buy such arguments. I believe instead that they will render us productive. For how can we achieve anything on an empty stomach?

"Much as I agree that we need to work hard to sustain our-selves, how can anyone expect us to be able to do so on an empty stomach? We need in the first instance food to provide us the needed energy. Friends, let us keep up pressure on the powers that be to initiate urgent actions to end our plight. Thanks for your attention."

***

Then followed a speaker from Europe:

"Ladies and gentlemen,
    "One of the cardinal goals of the UN is the maintenance of world peace.
    "In my view if the UN is geared towards the maintenance of world peace, poverty eradication must be accorded the topmost priority, for poverty is one of the main causes, if not the main cause, of conflicts and wars.
    "Indeed, as far as I am concerned, the UN's stated goal of ensuring world peace is meaningless unless abject poverty is eradicated from the surface of the world. The person who is des-perately poor may care less if the world is blown away in pieces through conflict.
    "By eradicating poverty, the world will be killing two birds with one stone.
    "Whereas the elimination of poverty will not lead to a com-plete end to war and warfare in our world, in our view it will lead to a significant reduction of conflict.
    "Much of the money it spends in peace missions could be saved and diverted to help fund other humanitarian activities such as disease eradication.
    "Long live the global forum of the poor!"

***

Finally, it was the turn of a delegate from Asia:

"Good morning, ladies and gentlemen,
"I send you greetings from the poor and deprived in Indonesia. Before I continue, allow me to offer a short introduction.
"I grew up in the Ciliwung slum settlement along the Cilliwung River in Jakarta.
"I want to highlight one particular developments of recent times in our community – namely slum tourism. It is a practice whereby tour guides take tourists around the slums to enable them to gain a first-hand impression of life in the area. Though not officially approved, it still happens. Those engaged in it argue that the trade permits visitors to the country the opportunity to have a glimpse of the other side of Indonesia.
"The question worth considering is: why should we permit human beings to live in such degrading circumstances in the first place, to provide others the opportunity to have a glimpse of how their fellow human beings are faring under such outrageous living conditions?
"Do we want such a state of affairs to continue in perpetuity? I am afraid that is what will happen if steps are not taken to address the situation,
"*We* the poor of this world are of the opinion that, whereas the UN is doing great work, as far as we are concerned it is not enough, so long as a quarter of the world's population live in squalor.
"We do not have all the answers. We are only making proposals which, we believe, are practicable and which, if implemented will lead to a reduction of world poverty. As one former leader of the world said, we are not looking left or right, we are looking straight ahead. We do not want any branding. Please do

not use words like 'left wing' or 'right wing', 'radical' or 'con-servative' to brand us. We are only fighting for our existence; we are Poverty Crusaders!

"To reiterate – our movement has nothing to do with politics, it has everything to do with our existence, the basic necessities of life, yes, with human dignity!

"Thank you very much for your attention."

Next, the chairwoman declared the session closed; delegates were to report to the groups they had been assigned to deliberate on various issues and report back to the full plenum the next day.

16

United Nations summit extraordinaire – Day 2

SPEECH 1

Proceedings began the next morning at a little past 9am. After a short welcoming speech by the chairwoman, Asia Group 1 was called upon to present the outcome of their deliberation:

"We were given the responsibility to deliberate on the matter of the initiation of a global welfare state; others may choose to call it the world benefit payment scheme.

"The wealth gap, ladies and gentlemen, is growing in various parts of the world, Asia being no exception.

"Let us take my own native Mumbai as an example. Indeed, it is easy to encounter a slum area just right behind the middle-class area, or even right behind the middle-upper, and upper-class area.

"The poor and disadvantaged of this world are disadvantaged when it comes to the mechanism or *modus operandi* of the free-market economy.

"In their dealings with each other, each country aims at making as much profit as possible.

"Whereas the system favours the wealthy countries, it places countries where most of us call home at a disadvantage. I am therefore calling for reform, indeed a rethink of the system.

"As a result of several factors, the details of which time will not permit me to dwell on, I and my fellow slum dwellers of Mumbai and elsewhere in the world are entrenched in poverty. Much as we would want to escape the depth of depravation and desperate need that we find ourselves in, sadly our efforts have not been successful.

"To avert the situation, we are hereby calling on the world community to pass an internationally binding law to introduce a global welfare state system in every country on Earth.

"Under the system, every resident of the world, irrespective of where they reside, will be guaranteed the minimum sum of money to ensure the barest standard of living.

"An independent international commission of experts will meet annually to set the figure. As a start, we are proposing a basic income of 2 dollars per day. This amount will be paid to whoever falls through the poverty net in developing countries.

"Indeed, in our view, every human being, every individual of our common human race, irrespective of race, colour, religion, political affiliation, etc., should be guaranteed the minimum standard of living to be set by a panel of experts.

"We shall leave the fine tuning of details in the implementation of such a scheme to international experts. Surely, a world that has the brains to send humans to the moon will not be unable to find experts to work out the details required for the successful implementation of such a scheme.

"This system does not call for the abolishing of social welfare schemes already in place in various countries. The global scheme, instead, is only intended to supplement the existing ones.

"Some may argue that with the introduction of the scheme, countries will fall short of their responsibilities to their citizens.

That is a legitimate fear. I am, however, confident that if proper measures are put in place by the experts, such a situation could be averted.

"Of course, such a revolutionary concept will, without doubt, face initial challenges. Surely, we do concede that we do not have all the answers.

"One thing we know, however. We the poor of the world want the world to understand that we cannot accept the present status quo.

"Indeed, we are calling on all men and women of goodwill to do all they can to ensure the world puts an end to the present untenable situation."

SPEECH 2

Next to follow was the Oceania Group made up of Australia and New Zealand. Below are excerpts from their presentation. We were asked them to deliberate on how to fund the proposed global welfare state system.

"Towards this goal, we call for the setting up of a Poverty Crusaders Fund to be administered by a Poverty Crusaders Authority, a body of experts – made up of men and women of exceptional probity and integrity.

"Such a body will be charged with the practical implementation of the global welfare system.

"Someone might ask, how will the proposed fund be resourced? I do not want to pre-empt the job of the teams assigned to coming up with proposals on how to generate income for the Poverty Crusaders Fund, so I will leave the stage for them."

SPEECH 3

Speech 3 was delivered by the Europe Group 1:

"We have identified the global arms trade as a possible source of funding for the proposed global welfare state system.

"Dear friends, ladies and gentlemen, during our deliberations, we were shell-shocked to realise how much money nations spend annually on arms.

"What causes my blood pressure to shoot up is the realisation that poor countries, yes, countries from where most of us originate, including the poorest of the poor, including countries whose citizens are dying of hunger and malnutrition – spend huge sums annually on arms.

"Imagine, my fellow delegates, what alien beings arriving on our planet would think of us if told that we were spending trillions of US dollars annually on arms, while at the same time, in serval parts of the globe, human beings have to forage through garbage dumps to earn their meagre living?

"I do not want to put words in their mouths. If I dare conjecture, they may probably think we are iron-hearted fellows with little or no feelings for the poor.

"I do indeed often ask myself, does the world need to defend itself from an alien invasion, yes, an invasion of foreign beings – from Mars, perhaps? Obviously, the answer is a big No. The truth is that vast sums of money are being spent by human beings to defend themselves from attack by other parts of humanity.

"Obviously, those who make decisions on the money spent – in our opinion wasted – do not reside in slums the likes of 'Sodom and Gomorrah' in Accra. Neither do their children face financial challenges in their education. If they did, they would consider making savings in the military expenditure with the goal of saving money to spend on the poor.

"We accepted in our deliberations the fact that we live in a dangerous world, an imperfect world that, from time to time, produces the likes of Adolf Hitler, Boko Haram, Isis, etc.

"It is nevertheless our conviction that nations have huge potential for cutting money spent on arms and defence. We call on our leaders to place emphasis on conflict prevention. If needs be, the UN should create as many conflict-prevention ambassadors as possible. Their duty would be to look out for conflicts and intervene at the least sign of conflict. Yes, they should act to prevent conflicts from breeding. Conflicts do not just descend from heaven. Often they breed for some time. Instead of waiting till it is too late to intervene, the UN should instead take early pre-emptive measures to defuse such conflicts. It may cost money, but it is our conviction that it will be cheaper than a full-blown conflict.

"Yes indeed, the goal should be to resort to diplomacy instead of war. To quote Winston Churchill: 'To jaw-jaw is always better than to war-war.'

"We are of the opinion many conflicts that have been fought in the past and continue to be fought would have been averted if that policy had been followed.

"It is our hope that one day all swords shall be turned into ploughshares. Until that happens, however, we are demanding that for every dollar nations spend on arms and other military equipment, a cent be paid into the Poverty Alleviation Fund.

"Besides taxing the purchasers, we are also demanding that for every dollar of profit made by manufacturers of weapons and other military armaments, a tax of a cent is paid into the Poverty Fund as well."

SPEECH 4

Next was the turn of the Africa Group 1.

"Before I present the outcome of our deliberations, I want to take the opportunity to introduce myself. I am a resident of the slums of Agbogbloshie, also known as 'Sodom and Gomorrah' in Accra.

"After completing my basic education, my parents were not in a position to pay for me to continue my education.

"Helping my parents on the field was out of the question for me. In the end I was lured by someone with the promise of a factory job in Accra. That turned out to be an empty promise. Eventually I ended up on the streets of Accra selling toilet rolls.

"I would really like to return to my village; unfortunately, I am stuck. The money I earn is enough to sustain me only for the day; in other words, I am living from hand to mouth, unable to save enough money to make it back to my village. Life in 'Sodom and Gomorrah' is a terrible existence. Excuse me for saying so, but we are existing there just like pigs – in squalor. Several of us share the same room. The place is infested with mosquitoes.

"Now to the outcome of our deliberations:

"Ladies and gentlemen, in our view, it is outrageous, yes, a disgrace, that humanity is sending people to explore space when on Earth, fellow human beings eke out their existence in slums and shanty towns like Nima in Accra, Ghana; Ajengule in Lagos, Nigeria; Neza (Mexico); Orangi Town in Karachi (Pakistan), etc. – dwelling in filth, squalor and absolute deprivation.

"Yes indeed, ladies and gentlemen, is it not a disgrace, is it not a shame on mankind, that we are sending humans to space when here on Earth people are living in dilapidated accommodation, indeed accommodation that without doubt is unfit for human habitation?

"Some may counter by saying the countries involved have earned their money and have the right to do whatever they wish with it.

"To that my response is simple: the materials they use in making their spaceships and jet planes, indeed belong to planet Earth and should be used to develop planet Earth, before using them for extra-terrestrial ventures.

"Yes indeed, in our opinion, humanity should first devote the resources on planet Earth towards solving the problems of our planet Earth before embarking on ventures into space.

"We demand that those who, despite the huge problems besetting mankind, still deem it expedient to invest the Earth's limited resources in space exploration, should be made to pay 0.1% of the resources they invest in space exploration into the Poverty Crusaders Fund."

SPEECH 5

Below is the contribution of the South America Group 2:

"We the slum dwellers of the world feel abandoned by all sides. The political classes of our respective countries are more interested in their own welfare than the plight of the poor.

"This applies also to the big players in the international political arena. Every country regards their citizens first, which, though legitimate, is not acceptable.

"We do not buy the idea the world is not in a position to eradicate poverty in its very abject form. It boils down in our view to the just distribution of wealth.

"As I researched for this speech, I came across an article published by CNN, the online edition of 21 January 2019, with the headline: 'The top 26 billionaires own $1.4 trillion – as much as 3.8 billion other people.'

"The article went on to state that, according to an Oxfam International report published the same day, the combined fortunes of the world's 26 richest individuals reached $1.4 trillion in 2018 – the same amount as the total wealth of the 3.8 billion poorest people.

"Ladies and gentlemen, please don't get me wrong. We have nothing against the rich; we wish them well.

"History is full of reports of where the so-called poor have risen up, against the wealthy, the bourgeoisies, in some cases in very violent ways. What was the outcome of such movements? They seized the property only to mess things up. We don't want to repeat such mistakes.

"Everyone who through sweat and dedication has built up wealth should be respected.

"Still, in my opinion the world cannot leave matters as they are.

"A situation where only 1% of the world's population controls half of the entire wealth of the world is, in my opinion, untenable!

"It is our hope that the world's political leaders will come up with a formula aimed at ensuring a fairer distribution of wealth.

"We cannot afford to wait on politicians. Well-fed and well-placed as they are, they may not recognise the urgency of the situation. We are therefore calling, without delay, for the imposition or introduction of a global poverty tax on the mega-rich. We leave it to the plenum to agree on a final figure. We for our part are proposing an annual tax of 0.1% to be levied on any resident of the globe with an estimate worth of a 100 million US dollars and beyond. We arrived at this figure after a lengthy debate. In the end we reached the consensus that anyone worth 100 million US dollars and above has established enough financial security to enable that individual to contribute towards lifting others from poverty without feeling the pinch.

"No one should get us wrong. We are not in any way jealous of the wealthy. If through various circumstances or means – hard work, inheritance, or other circumstances – they have attained considerable wealth, we are humbly appealing to them to share a tiny fraction of it with those who, for various reasons, have fallen through the net.

SPEECH 6

Below is the contribution of the Europe Group 2:

"Dear friends from the rest of the world.

"Before I make my point, I want you to know that, just as it was reported by our friend from New York yesterday, poverty exists in the rich industrialised world as well as in the rest of the world. Of course, the situation in North America and Western Europe can in no way be compared to that of so-called third-world or developing countries; nevertheless, it must be borne in mind that several factors can lead one into poverty.

"In my case, I fell victim to the wicked and greedy capitalist system entrenched in my country. To cut a long story short – I got a job. I took a mortgage. The owner of my company moved the company elsewhere, leading me to become unemployed. As a result, I was incapable of paying for my mortgage. One default payment warning after the other reached me. Finally, I was forced out of my property on a cold winter day.

"Now, I turn to the resolution passed by the Europe group. These days everyone is talking about global warming. The question that needs to be addressed is – who bears the major blame for the current state of affairs? Not you, my poor friends from the slums of developing countries.

"Which one of you has ever dreamt of flying your children around the globe on holidays? Even if someone donated a ticket to enable you for example to travel from Ajengule to visit Disneyland, which embassy will be prepared to grant you a visa?

"Which one of you can afford a high-powered, high fuel-consuming vehicle that blasts great amounts of pollutants into the atmosphere?

"We, the poor of Europe, are calling for the imposition of a 0.1% global warming tax on the annual profits of companies producing environmental polluters or involved in activities that directly or indirectly lead to environmental pollution – automobile and aircraft manufacturers, petroleum exploration, etc.

"The money raised will be paid into the Poverty Crusaders Fund."

SPEECH 7

African Group 2 speaker contributed as follows:

"Mr Chairman, ladies and gentlemen:

"I bring you warm greetings from the slum dwellers of Kibera, Nairobi, Kenya.

"I am reporting on the outcome of deliberations of the Africa Group. Before I do so, I want to pass a comment:

"There is a nomenclature for a poor person: 'Poor No Friend'; well, at least for this momentous period in time, the attention of the world is focused on us, the poor. We need to take advantage of the huge publicity to raise our profile. The world may forget us tomorrow. So, ladies and gentlemen, let us grasp the opportunity of the moment and make the world take notice of us. Well, they may forget us tomorrow, but at leaﬆ today we are the talk of the world.

"I am so excited at the opportunity to speak. I would have liked to speak for at leaﬆ two hours. Indeed, how do you expect me to recount all the woes of the poor in my country in the short time at my disposal?

"I do appreciate the need for me to be brief so as to give the other speakers the opportunity to present their cases.

"I do not want to be as greedy as some of our politicians who, by their actions, create the impression that their greed is insatiable.

"In our deliberations, my group have not loﬆ sight of the fact that a good deal of our countries are blessed with massive natural resources – oil, gas, coal. Some also boaﬆ, in addition, fertile land. The queﬆion one may ask is, why are such countries poor in the presence of abundant resources?

"Yes indeed, the legitimate queﬆion worth asking is – where has all the money gone? The answer of course is not farfetched – greedy elements – both within and without – our countries have teamed up to plunder our wealth.

Of course, we do expect those who inveﬆ in our economies to earn decent returns on their inveﬆments. What we are lamenting is the failure of such companies, local as well as multinational, to pay the tax due from their activities to the countries from where the profits were made.

"There is also no secret that the huge sums of monies from the poor and impoverished countries of the world are looted and deposited in international banks by corrupt politicians and business entities.

"This practice of taking money from the national coffers of poor countries to deposit in banks in wealthy countries, yes robbing the poor to keep the rich even richer, in our view amounts to crimes againﬆ humanity.

"We are calling on well-meaning political figures worldwide to put measures in place to prevent such greedy, cold-hearted individuals from depositing their ill-gotten wealth in their countries.

"We are calling on the UN, the highest international legal authority on Earth, without delay, to enact international internally legally binding laws to check this wanton greed. In particular, we are calling for the UN, without delay, to classify the plundering of the coffers of a nation – whether by locals or foreigners – as 'a crime against humanity'.

"How else should we classify the callous deeds, the wanton deeds of the heartless uncaring, insensitive, stony-hearted individuals and companies against the impoverished populations of such countries?

"Agreed, such individuals are not directly committing genocide. Their wicked deeds, however, directly or indirectly contribute to want, malnutrition, deprivation or inaccessibility of medical care, which in turn leads to the untimely deaths of millions!"

SPEECH 8

Below is the contribution of the North America Group:

"To prosecute those arrested under the proposed global poverty arrest warrant, we are calling for the UN to set up an international tribunal similar to the already existing International Court of Justice to be charged with the prosecution of politicians, business executives, multinational corporations and other individuals, suspected of crimes that fall under the crimes already stated.

"There is a saying that when persuasion fails, force is applied. Indeed, over the last several years, in my country, there have been proven cases of government officials, governors, etc., blatantly looting the coffers of the state. What happens when such individuals are exposed? Almost nothing! It is therefore time for an impartial international persecutory authority to take over. Thank you very much for your attention."

SPEECH 9

The following is a report from the deliberations of the South America 2 Group.

"Just by way of introduction, I am from Sao Paolo, Brazil. Many of you no doubt associate Brazil with football. I was a talented footballer until I fractured my ankle. Well, if I had not, I might have ended up as a football millionaire. I get the impression, Providence wanted me to be part of this movement, so I was prevented from making inroads in my football profession."

The hall burst into laughter.

"Our group engaged ourselves with the distribution of wealth on our planet. Thanks to some of the brilliant heads amongst us who helped us research the internet, the following became clear:

"The population of the world is currently around 6 billion individuals. Out of that number over 25% live in abject poverty, having to exist on virtually nothing or at the very maximum on 1.30 US dollars daily. Another 25% live on less than 2.50 US dollars daily.

"To put it another way, about half of the world's population, all of us present included, live in poverty.

"We have for a while believed our own politicians would help rectify the situation. From the look of things, however, there is no indication, that will happen in the foreseeable future.

"There is therefore an urgent need for us to step out of our inactivity and start campaigning, fighting, indeed agitating for our rights.

"As a first step, we are calling for the creation of a seat at the UN for a representative of the poor and deprived. How can the UN be regarded as a humanitarian body representing the world, when there is no direct representative for 25–50% of the world's population?

"Others may argue that we are indirectly represented by our various countries. Well, personally speaking, I don't feel represented, for I do not even know who represents my country.

"We are calling not for the creation of an ordinary seat; we are demanding instead that the *UN Seat for the Poor*, as we are proposing to call it, is accorded a veto power status.

"Ladies and gentlemen, the UN Security Council in its present form, is a relic of the immediate post-World War II situation and not reflective of the present world population.

"Dear friends, World War II ended almost 75 years ago, didn't it? The world has changed considerably since then.

"Is it too much, ladies and gentlemen, for a seat representing between 25% and 50% of the world's population be accorded a veto power status?

"Equipped with a veto power, such a seat will enable us to play a vital role in steering the affairs of the UN.

"Finally, to ensure that the veto power assigned to the Security Council is not unduly thwarted by vested interests aimed at frustrating the rights of the poor, we call for the introduction of a system whereby an objection by a veto power country can be overturned by 75% of Security Council members.

"This, it is our hope, will avert a situation whereby other security members could connive to frustrate the efforts of our future representative to fight for our interests."

SPEECH 10

The final speech was delivered by a representative of Asia Group 2:

"Before I make my contribution, I want to seize this opportunity to send the warm greetings of the slum dwellers of Calcutta to our friends from little Mpintimpi.

"Your action in bringing the pitiful plight of the poor of the world before the courts of the powers that be has contributed to this meeting, a meeting that has helped to put the poor of our common planet in the limelight.

"As I made my way to the meeting, I was astounded by the large numbers of satellite transmission vans positioned in and around the UN headquarters buildings. It is a testimony to how much attention this campaign has garnered worldwide.

"My country, India, is usually praised by the world press as being the largest democracy on Earth! During the last general election an estimated 900 million people took part. In the end, it took several days to complete the exercise.

"Of course, I am not calling for a dictatorship in India. Democracy, in all its weakness, should always be preferred over a dictatorship.

"But what is the use in casting my vote every couple of years if I and my family continue to live an existence that is below human dignity?

"I would indeed, have wished that the world press that heaped praise on my country during elections would spend a night in our slum hotel instead of the 4- to 5-star hotels during their stay here to report on such elections.

"Dear friends, ladies and gentlemen, we need to keep the momentum of the hour going; yes, we don't have to allow things to return back to normalcy after this meeting.

"Having said that by way of introduction, I want to make known to you the outcome of the deliberations of our group:

"To maintain and sustain public awareness, to ensure our campaign does not fade away from public consciousness, we are calling for the establishment of what we term the Global Week of Action for the Poor.

"During the week of action, it should be obligatory for the president or head of state of each country on Earth to spend a few days interacting with the poor in their slums, in their delipidated dwellings. They should not visit there only during the daytime; they should also spend at least a night sleeping there.

"During their stay, they should not expect any preferential treatment; no, they would live just like anyone else in the settlement. Indeed, apart from having access to their usual security regime – they won't enjoy any privileges that are not available to the residents.

"For example, they will receive the same meal (if any), drink the same water we drink (treated or non-treated) and sleep like anyone else – whether on a bed, a mat spread on the floor, or the bare floor! They won't have the right to sleep under mosquito nets – unless the residents have access to such a facility prior to the arrival of the prominent visitor.

"Every year, the UN will be required, during the Global Week of the Poor, to place its facilities in New York at our disposal to offer us the opportunity to take stock of the state of our movement."

17

Global march of the poor and downtrodden

The global Poverty Crusaders march took place the next day as planned. Starting from the UN headquarters building, the large procession, which was estimated at around a hundred thousand participants, marched through the route mapped out by the city authorities to Central Park in Manhattan.

To my surprise, I was selected to deliver the closing speech, which I have reproduced below:

"Dear friends, ladies and gentlemen,

"I am privileged to be accorded the honour to deliver the closing speech to this historic meeting. Over the last three days, we have got the world to pay attention, indeed to let the world know that we are part of the human community, that not only do we have the right to be on planet Earth, but also that we have the right to decent living – not in luxury, but at least the minimum standard required to ensure a decent human existence.

"Could anyone have imagined a few months ago that the poor in the slums of the world could be interviewed on some of the leading news channels on Earth, that we could actually be granted an audience by the UN secretary-general, as well as the UN Security Council, and that we could meet on the premises of the UN?!

"The world is listening, the world has taken notice, the world has been made aware of our plight. Thanks to your co-ordinated efforts, that is exactly what has happened.

"We should not rest on our oars, though.

"I need not mention the fact that human beings have the tendency to forget. Today in the headlines, tomorrow forgotten – that could happen should we relax in our efforts.

"In order to remain in the limelight, in order not to be forgotten, we need to keep up the pressure. How are we going to do that?

"In this connection, I would like to draw your attention to the Greenpeace movement.

"They have achieved this through various means.

"Indeed, they have over the years resorted to various nonviolent direct actions, some spectacular, some less spectacular, as a way of stopping environmental crimes from happening. Though such actions are primarily aimed at preventing environmental abuse or crimes from happening, the spectacular nature of such actions also helped to keep them in the limelight.

"We need, my good friends, to emulate their strategy to help us achieve our goals. What kind of actions do I envisage?

"I can think of several. For now I will highlight only two of them.

"Before I do that, allow me to pass a comment.

"Winston Churchill, the famous British politician and World War II hero, is quoted as saying 'It is better to jaw-jaw than to war-war'.

"In keeping with his thinking, we for now will adopt a jaw-jaw approach – words, arguments, persuasion – to get the world to meet the demands outlined in our 10-point manifesto.

"If after all our 'jaw-jaw' efforts nothing is forthcoming, we shall be forced to embark on a 'war-war' strategy. Of course, we are not going to take up arms and head for war – may God forbid!

"Instead, in line with the Greenpeace movement actions I alluded to earlier on, we shall embark on peaceful, though spectacular, protest actions aimed at exerting pressure on the powers that be to act on our demands.

"Much talk these days centres on climate change and global warming.

"In this regard, I want to remind the global community, world leaders included, about the vital role played by the huge forests, the likes of the Amazon, Congo, Indonesia, etc., in maintaining the ecological balance of the planet.

"I need not remind you, my dear friends, that the majority of the poor live in or near these huge forests, which can be described as the oxygen reservoir of planet Earth.

"Therein lies our chance, ladies and gentlemen! If the wealthy of the world refuse to contribute towards lifting us out of abject poverty, we will use the huge forest reserves at our disposal as a bargaining chip.

"How will that happen in practice, some may want to know?

"To begin with, we shall dispatch a note of warning to leading world figures such as the presidents of the US, the EU, China, Russia and the UN secretary-general, setting a deadline for the rapid implementation of a universal welfare state system, which, as you are aware, is based on a minimum daily payment of 2 US dollars to those who meet the set criteria.

"Failure to meet our deadline will leave us with no option other than initiating a global protest action.

"The first action will involve hundreds and thousands of the poor resident in and around the major forests of the globe arming themselves with axes, chainsaws, machetes and inflammable liquid, and cutting down as many of the trees as they are able to and then setting the forests ablaze!

"My dear friends, you cannot even imagine the effect such a threat could have – a catastrophic effect on an already damaged world climate and especially on the residents there.

"Soon environmental as well as human rights activists in major cities such as Berlin, London, Paris, New York, Tokyo, will pour on the streets in their hundreds of thousands to support our cause and urge their leaders to support our legitimate call to end global abject poverty.

"Apart from playing the climate card, another card we could play is that of immigration.

"In this regard, we could make use of the tendency for some of the residents of industrialised countries to grow paranoid when it comes to the issue of immigration.

"It is strange but true that residents in Western cities like Berlin, Paris, London and New York, a population group that have ongoing contact with immigrants in their respective countries, are usually unconcerned by their presence.

"On the other hand, residents living in remote areas, who may never come into contact with newcomers, have a tendency to grow paranoid about their presence.

"Indeed, the mere sight of a ship in the Mediterranean, far from the borders of Europe, carrying migrants, which may or may not actually make it to the shores of Europe, let alone end up settling anywhere near them, may cause such individuals sleepless nights over concerns Europe could be deluged by immigrants!

"We could exploit that irrational behaviour of the natives of the rich nations for our cause by organising what I will describe as a 'south–north exodus' of vast dimensions.

"This will involve organising a huge number of mostly vulnerable residents of the slums of our places of residence and bringing them to the borders of the rich countries to beg them permission to enter their respective countries.

"It is part of human nature that we usually have sympathy for human suffering, especially when it involves starving children, the handicapped, women and the elderly.

"Indeed, despite their concern about the influx of migrants into their countries, TV and other media pictures depicting scenes of suffering of such groups of individuals at the borders will exert huge pressure on politicians to act to end the suffering.

"We shall take advantage of this innate quality of normal human beings to empathise with human suffering to our advantage.

"In this connection, there will be two main action zones:

"The first will involve our compatriots in South America; the other will involve those in Africa.

"Our friends in South America will require a minimum of a hundred trains for their action. The chartered trains will be filled to the last seat by children, the handicapped, women and the elderly and head for the Mexico–US border.

"The Africa campaign will require hundreds if not thousands of trucks. They will pick up impoverished and malnourished children, highly pregnant women, the blind, the handicapped, the maimed, the elderly from all over the continent and transport them to the Mediterranean coast in Libya. As we are aware, from there we would have to overcome the obstacle of the Mediterranean Sea in order to get to Europe.

"Towards that goal, we will have to organise an armada of about a hundred seaworthy ships to transport then to Continental Europe, not forgetting the British Isles. How do we come by the required funds, you might ask? No problem, my friends. There are a good proportion of residents of Europe and elsewhere in the world – human right activists, anti-capitalist groups, environmental activists – who will readily support our action, either by placing ships at our disposal or donating money to enable us to charter the ships needed for the campaign.

"We live in an age of social media; we will take advantage of that. Simultaneous to our action, we shall start a social media campaign to get our message through to the rest of the world.

"The fear of destabilising their societies, indeed causing social uproar, will certainly force politicians to act, indeed to take steps to meet our demands.

"Ladies and gentlemen, let us not give up.

"Fighting to end abject poverty, making sure no human being exists in conditions that fall far below the acceptable level of human dignity, is a cause worth fighting for.

"May Almighty God bless our effort.

"Thank you very much for your attention."

The speech was greeting with a standing ovation that appeared to be unending. It took a while for calm to be restored to the gathering.

Finally, the chairperson took the microphone. Announcing that the UN Secretariat had agreed to the request to permit an annual gathering of the movement at the premises of the UN and that a meeting would be held at the same time the following year, she read out the final 10-point action plan agreed upon, which is reproduced below.

18

A radical plan to inflict a death blow to want and deprivation

After three days of intense deliberations on various aspects of global poverty, the extraordinary meeting of the poor and underprivileged of this world came to an end. A communique outlining a 10-point action plan aimed at poverty alleviation was adopted as follows:

We the poor, destitute, underprivileged of the world, struggling every day to make ends meet, hereby declare our demands as follows:

1) We demand the mandatory introduction of a global welfare state system in every member state of the UN to ensure that a basic minimum standard of living, set by an independent commission of experts, is guaranteed for every resident of planet Earth, irrespective of their places of residence.

2) We call for the setting up of a common poverty crusaders fund to be administered by a panel of experts – men and women of high standing and integrity – to ensure the practical implementation of the global welfare state system.

3) We are calling for the introduction of a 0.1% (zero point one percent) global tax on arms' sales worth over half a million

US dollars. It will be a two-way taxation affecting those who sell as well as those who purchase arms. The money levied will be paid directly into the common poverty crusaders fund.

4) We demand the introduction of a global space exploration tax.

In our opinion, humanity should first devote available resources towards the advancement of planet Earth towards solving the myriad of problems facing mankind, before venturing into space.

Aware that we cannot impose our will on others, we demand that those who, despite the huge problems besetting mankind, still deem it expedient to invest our limited resources towards space exploration, should be made to pay 0.01% tax on the expenditure of their exploration into the poverty crusaders fund.

5) Global green tax (aka global environment protection levy).

We hereby call for the imposition of 0.1% global warming tax to be imposed by companies/states/organisations generally identified as environmental polluters – automobile, aircraft, petroleum exploration, etc. Such moneys will flow into the poverty crusaders fund.

6) Global poverty tax on the mega-rich for poverty alleviation.

Whereas we are not jealous of the rich, we still consider it fair to demand that any individual worth 100 million US dollars pay an annual tax of 0.01% of their wealth, into the global poverty alleviation fund.

7) Poverty crusaders arrest warrant.

We are calling for the UN Security Council to enact an internationally binding GPAAW legislation, which will make it obligatory for nations to arrest any individuals accused of plundering the coffers of their respective countries of origin to face justice.

8) Poverty crusaders tribunal.

We are calling for the UN to set up a tribunal to prosecute those arrested anywhere in the world for plundering, looting, embezzling funds of their respective countries of origin and thereby contributing to the entrenching of poverty in their respective countries.

9) We demand a collective veto power for the poor of the world at the United Nations. This, in our view, is the only way the voice of the poor who make up more than half of the world's population can be heard.

10) Global poverty week.

We have no illusions that poverty and want can be completely eradicated from the surface of the globe. To keep on reminding the world about the existence of poverty, indeed to prevent the theme from fading from the thoughts of the world community, we are calling for a week to be set aside each year to deliberate the matter and take appropriate steps to fight it. During the global poverty week, various fund-raising activities will be undertaken with the goal to raising funds through donations and other activities for the global poverty fund.

Thus the historic summit of the global poor and disadvantaged at the UN Headquarters in New York came to an end.

With much optimism for the future, everyone headed for their various destinations.

19

From dream to bitter reality

B uoyed up by our success, we headed back home congratulat-
ing ourselves on our achievement, indeed for bringing our
issues to the attention of the rest of the world.

I decided not to return directly to my base in England, but
rather to accompany the rest of the delegation to report back to
the Chief and the people of the village.

We would have liked to have travelled straight from Accra to
the village—but no! Following the worldwide publicity we had
triggered, the matter had no longer become our own, but rather
a national event.

A welcoming Reception ceremony was said to have been or-
ganized to welcome us back. We would be met at the airport by
the chief of staff and sent to Jubilee House for a short meeting
with the President.

Our understanding was that he had already set up a task force
to explore avenues to implement the benefit system in Ghana.

I followed the progress of our flight by way of the interactive map views and destination information of the in-flight en-
tertainment system, displayed on the back of the seat in front of
me. Thanks to the interactive map I did not feel like I was lost
somewhere in outer space, but knew approximately where I was.

As we were just about halfway through crossing the Sahara
Desert at a height of over 10000 metres above ground level, suddenly the plane began to shake violently!

"We have encountered severe turbulence," the Captain announced. "Please fasten your seat belts. Cabin crew, please return to your seats!"

Just then the aircraft dropped considerably, sending cold chills down my spine.

Not believing my eyes, I saw several passengers who might have been asleep and therefore did not hear the announcement to fasten their seat belts, literally flying towards the ceiling, the luggage compartments and aisles of the airplane.

I had encountered turbulences in previous flights, but this particular one seemed to be playing in an upper league.

"This is going to be the end!" I murmured.

As the pilot struggled to keep the aircraft in the air, suddenly I heard a clanging noise. Initially the sound appeared to be quite distant. Gradually it drew closer. I turned in the direction it seemed to be coming from with the aim of identifying whatever was causing it. At that moment, my eyes opened. The surroundings became familiar—I was in my bedroom! It then dawned on me that I had been in a dream!!

"Damn it!" I said to myself! I had thought that I, together with the residents of my little village, had taken a bold step towards the eradication of world poverty—only to realize it was all in a dream!

EPILOGUE

Poverty Crusaders, here we come!

Inspired by the dream that I have just shared with the rest of the world, I have resolved to do what I can to alleviate, if not completely eradicate, world poverty.

As a first step, I have established the Poverty Crusaders, a charitable organisation, to serve as the vehicle through which efforts towards the realisation of my goals of poverty alleviation will be channelled.

Dear reader, you are heartily invited to come on board, indeed to join efforts towards helping the millions of the poor of this world. Whereas I have no illusions that poverty will ever be completely eradicated from the surface of the earth, it is my belief that with concerted efforts and the needed goodwill, we can make a difference, however small.

For further information concerning the activities of the charity and how you could be of help, please visit the website www. povertycrusaders.org

Lightning Source UK Ltd.
Milton Keynes UK
UKHW022122021119
352795UK00004B/20/P